S0-BHW-837

A STUDY IN STONE

Michael
Campling

The Devonshire Mysteries
Book I

Shadowstone
Books

THE AWKWARD SQUAD – THE HOME OF PICKY READERS:

All members get a free mystery book plus a starter collection:

mikeycampling.com/freebooks

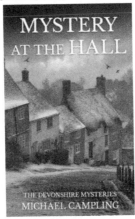

CHAPTER 1

Dartmoor

Dan Corrigan peered out through the grime-streaked windscreen and clung tight to the steering wheel of the old Toyota RAV4 as the car bounced and shuddered over the potholed tarmac. He'd been driving for hours, stopping only when absolutely necessary, but now, as the sun swept towards the horizon, he needed to get out of the damned car.

There's nowhere to pull off this bloody lane, he thought. *Not even a lay-by.* He had to press on, but there was no sign of his destination, only the endless single-track road that twisted and turned, meandering its wilful way across the countryside. And as the last of the early evening light faded, the tall hedges on either side pressed in on him, the probing fingers of crooked branches clutching at the car's wing mirrors. Impossibly, the road seemed to be getting narrower all the time, and as he turned a corner, the road rose steeply, dwindling into the distance.

"This can't be right," he muttered to the empty car. "I must've taken a wrong turn."

But the app on his phone had distinctly told him to take this road, and just as he slowed the car to a crawl, he caught sight of a light in the distance: the faint orange glow of a streetlight flickering into life. It was the most civilized thing he'd seen for the last forty-five minutes, and a faint hope stirred in his heart. Cautiously, he pressed his foot on the accelerator, and ignoring the rattles and creaks of complaint coming from somewhere beneath the car, he drove up the steep incline.

I don't believe it, he thought. But there, caught in the glare from the headlights, a white sign peeped out from the hedgerow:

WELCOME TO EMBERVALE
PLEASE DRIVE SLOWLY

"If I go much slower, I'll grind to a halt," he grumbled, but finally, he was in the right place, and he eased back on the accelerator, looking out for a street sign as the hedgerows gave way to houses and tidy front gardens.

But if the street was labelled in any way, he must've missed it, and there was no one in sight to ask for directions, so he drove on, trying to read the nameplates that seemed to adorn each house, no two in the same style.

His phone told him to make a right turn, and Dan obeyed, steering the Toyota into a side street, and here, at last, was the house he'd been looking for, its quaint slate sign announcing it to be: *The Old Shop*.

As his sister had promised, the house was fronted by a square patch of rough gravel that served as a parking space, and as the Toyota's tyres crunched over the uneven surface, he looked up at the cream coloured cottage. Although the house was in darkness, it looked pleasant enough, and it would certainly be more than big enough for his needs.

Not bad, he told himself. *Not bad at all*. Killing the engine, he made sure that the headlights were off, then he climbed from the car, arching his back. The cottage's keys were attached to the car key along with half a dozen smaller keys that he'd have to figure out later, and he headed for the front door, anxious to get his stuff shifted inside so that he could sit down, attack the meagre stock of groceries that he'd bought on the way, and possibly crack open a bottle of beer.

But as he struggled to slide the key into the unfamiliar lock, someone called out from behind him:

"Hello, there."

Dan glanced over his shoulder. "Hi." He tried the key again, but it wouldn't turn.

"Nice evening," the stranger said, apparently in no hurry to leave. "I was just on my way to the pub."

"Okay," Dan replied absently. "I see." There was another, very similar key on the bunch, so perhaps he'd made a mistake. He tried it, but this one was even worse. It didn't even fit the slot.

The stranger chuckled. "This always seems to happen. I think the lock must be a touch tricky. If I see a new arrival, I usually tell them to try the back door."

Dan stopped what he was doing and faced the man properly. "Thanks. I'll do that." He hesitated. "How do you know that? About the lock?"

The man hooked his thumb over his shoulder to indicate the next house on the street. "I'm a neighbour. I've lived here for a few years, so I've seen lots of people arrive here for a holiday. Not so many recently, though. Are you here for long?"

Dan shook his head. "I'm not on holiday, just taking a break from London. This is my sister's house. She's been abroad for a long time. Usually, she lets it out, but as you say, not so much these days." He forced a smile. When was this man going to walk away and let him get on with moving in? Did he have nothing better to do?

"Oh, your sister," the man said. "Yes, I think we've met. I can see the resemblance now."

"Really?" Dan looked more closely at this strangely perceptive man. People usually remarked on how dissimilar he was from his sister: she was fair-skinned, he had a ruddy complexion; she was blonde, his mop of thick hair was dark; her nose was elegantly petite, his was broad and strong. On the other hand, it was a fact noticed by few, that both he and his sister had the same grey eyes.

"Yes." The man stepped closer, his hand extended for a shake. "I'm Alan, by the way. Alan Hargreaves."

"Hi. I'm Dan." They shook hands. Alan's grip was firm, and Dan realized that his neighbour was younger than he'd first supposed. They were probably about the same age, but Alan's clothes were dull to the point of being dowdy.

"So, how long will you be with us?" Alan asked. "One week? Two?"

"I haven't made my mind up," Dan replied. "I'll see how it goes."

"Right. Well…" Alan shifted his weight from one foot to the other. "As I said, I'm just off to the pub. They have a decent selection of ales if you're at a loose end while you're here."

Dan made a show of tilting his head from side to side as if weighing up the possibilities. "Thanks, but I'll probably get settled in."

"Okay, but if you change your mind, it's just along Fore Street. You can't miss it, it's the only pub in the village. The Wild Boar is its official name, but most people just call it The Boar." Alan smiled. "Personally, I think of it as *The Interminable*."

Dan found himself laughing. "The Interminable Bore. Very good."

"Mind you, I don't say that to the landlord's face. Kevin is all right once you get to know him, but..." Alan waggled his hand. "Bit of a temper."

"I'll bear that in mind, but I doubt I'll try it. Not really my thing."

Alan lowered his eyebrows as if sizing Dan up. "Of course, it's not like the trendy cocktail bars of London, but we like it. It's a good place to meet the locals. They run a quiz every now and then, and there's a meat raffle every Friday."

"Oh my God," Dan breathed. "Is that a real thing?"

"Yes. It's not something I'd make up, trust me."

Dan shook his head. "Listen, I don't mean to be rude, but I've got a lot to unpack, so it was nice to meet you, Alan, but I'd better get to it."

"No worries. Enjoy your stay." Alan shot him a genuine smile then marched away, whistling a jaunty tune under his breath.

When was the last time I heard someone whistle? Dan asked himself. He looked around at the silent houses, imagining for a moment that he'd travelled back in time. But this was good. Peace and quiet. Solitude. It was what he wanted. What he *needed*. And taking out his phone to use as a flashlight, he went in search of the cottage's back door.

***

Dan stared at the television. Four channels. *Four.* No satellite, definitely no cable, and apparently, no broadband. There was a telephone, but no router.

"What the hell am I going to do?" he muttered. He'd shifted his few belongings into the house, and he'd even hung his shirts in the wardrobe. His food supplies were basic, but he'd knocked together a quick veggie chilli and wolfed it down. Then he'd thrown himself onto the sofa in the small lounge and opened a bottle of beer. He was looking forward to that drink, but the German lager hadn't been in the fridge for long enough, and it tasted sour and gassy. He took a couple of sips then put the bottle on the coffee table and slumped in his seat, the evening stretching out before him, long and desolate. There was nothing worth watching on the TV, so he turned it off with the remote, and a sudden

4

silence filled the room. He tilted his head, straining his ears, but he couldn't hear a single sound. Not even a distant car.

Dan drummed his fingers on the sofa's armrests, then he pulled out his wallet. Yes, he had some cash: enough for a pint or two. The wonders of contactless payments may not have made it to this little village, but the prices around here would be much lower than in London, wouldn't they?

I should stay in, get some rest, he told himself. *Yes, I should definitely have an early night. Definitely.*

He stood, straightening his shirt, then he strode across the room and hurried through the kitchen. Ignoring the washing up, he grabbed his jacket from the hook by the door, and a moment later, he was striding along the quiet street. At the corner, he turned right and was rewarded with the sign for Fore Street. The pub was not far away, its painted sign swinging in the breeze, and as Dan marched along the road, without really meaning to, he began to whistle.

CHAPTER 2

Exeter

Dan Corrigan stopped in the narrow street and took out his phone. According to the map, he was just a few minutes away from the coffee shop, but this wasn't the first time today that it had promised such hopeful news. Indeed, at one point, the software had cheerfully announced that he'd reached his destination, but Dan, staring at the storefronts on offer (a tattoo parlour, a hairdresser, and some sort of retro videogame emporium) had been inclined to disagree.

Why had he even agreed to come here today? *Because I need to make the house bearable*, he reminded himself. The cottage, though comfortable enough, was sadly lacking in terms of creature comforts, and one or two essentials were missing as well. The only sharp knife in the kitchen was so flimsy that it was a danger to anyone who dared to wield it, the can opener was only mildly more effective than a swift jab with a chisel, and the cafetiere! The metal filter was so worn and bent that not only did it fail to contain the ground coffee, but it seemed to fire it upwards in swirling jets of foaming liquid that sputtered from the spout to soak anyone unfortunate enough to be in the vicinity. So when, in the pub the night before, Alan had suggested that he could pick up the things he needed on a trip to Exeter, even offering to show him around, Dan had agreed to go along, and in a moment of madness, he'd offered to drive.

So far, he'd managed to buy a decent cafetiere and a chef's knife, complete with a good-sized chopping board, as well as one or two other useful items, but he was rapidly running out of patience. Alan might have sensed this, because when they'd passed a secondhand bookshop, he'd dived inside, leaving Dan to his own devices for a while.

Dan had welcomed the chance to wander around getting his bearings, but now, the ghost of the golden ale from the night before had appeared to haunt him, and he had to have coffee—good coffee, and lots of it—but his damned phone had confounded him.

See Exeter and die, he thought balefully, staring along the cobbled street. *Die of thirst, die of boredom, die of confusion.*

"Are you all right there?"

Dan turned on his heel. The middle-aged woman was studying him with polite concern. She was well dressed, in a long black coat and kitten heels, and her hair, streaked with silver, had been expertly cut in a style that suited her extremely well. For a moment, it struck Dan as very odd that the woman should feel confident in approaching a strange man in a quiet backstreet, but it was the middle of the afternoon, and although the street was quiet, the main shopping drag was just a few yards away. *Plus, this isn't London*, he reminded himself. *They do things differently here.*

He forced a smile. "Yes, fine thank you. Just checking my phone." He waggled the device in the air unnecessarily. "You know how it is. Never switched off. Never a moment's peace."

"Oh dear." There was sympathy in her pale blue eyes. "Only, you look a bit lost. And to be honest, if you carry on down here, you'll be heading off the beaten track. I'm on my way to work, but most people don't venture down this way."

"Right. Okay." Dan's grin felt fixed to his lips. *Go on*, he told himself. *Admit that you're lost. Ask for directions.* But it was no use; he couldn't bring himself to do it. "Well, in that case, I'll go back the way I came."

The woman didn't say anything. She just watched him as if expecting more.

"Cheers," Dan said, then he turned and walked away without looking back.

The main street was depressing. Yes, there were coffee shops here, but they were the franchises he could find on any street in the western hemisphere. And he didn't just want an indifferent mug of brown stuff, he wanted carefully selected organically grown beans, roasted in some obscure way over a wood fire by a fairly paid Ghanaian, ground to a tolerance of one hundredth of a millimetre, and brewed by a barista with theatrical facial hair and a deep knowledge of non-pressurised baskets. He wanted artisanal. He wanted *COFFEE*.

And he was damned if he was going to settle for anything less.

The painstaking search on his phone had shown him the top ten coffee shops in Exeter, and he would try once again to find the place holding the top spot: The Aquifer Café. And this time, he *would* succeed.

Walking faster now, he traced his path back to the place he'd left his...what was Alan, exactly? A neighbour, certainly, but a friend? They'd only met the day before, but they'd hit it off over a pint in the pub, and despite having nothing whatsoever in common, the time had flown past in his company. *I don't know*, Dan decided. *Is it worth my while making friends around here?* Probably not. He wouldn't stay in Devon for long. Soon, he'd feel like heading back to the city. London. The place where you couldn't heave half a brick without hitting at least half a dozen baristas, and all of them masters in the art of the consistent crema. True, most of the baristas he knew had doctorates in Medieval Literature or some such, but at least they'd found gainful employment. They were the lucky ones.

Dan halted outside the secondhand bookshop and peered in through the window. Why was it so easy to see inside? Why wasn't the glass streaked with dust and dirt? *Different*, he thought bitterly. *Whoever said variety is the spice of life, was an idiot.* A movement caught his eye. There, inside, a man had raised his hand in acknowledgement. Alan.

Dan hurried into the shop, attracting stares from the surprisingly large number of customers. *What? Am I wearing a sign?* Perhaps it was his speed that attracted attention. No one around here was ever in a hurry. No one. And it was driving him crazy.

"What's up?" Alan asked as Dan marched between the cramped rows of shelves. "Everything all right?"

"Don't you start," Dan shot back.

Alan's face fell, the hurt look in his eyes a silent rebuke.

"Sorry," Dan mumbled. "Er, how are you doing? Found anything good?"

Alan wrinkled his nose. "Not really. Shelves full of bestsellers. No good to me."

"But, surely, if they're bestsellers, they ought to be worth reading, shouldn't they?"

"You'd think." Alan halfheartedly pulled a paperback from the shelf then pushed it straight back. "No. I don't want bubble-gum for the mind. I'm looking for something a bit different. Something with a bit of weight."

Dan pointed to a shelf labelled *Fantasy.* "Those are pretty thick."

"No, no. I don't mean physically heavy. I mean something a bit..." Alan circled his hand in the air.

"More challenging? More intellectual."

"Just *better*," Alan corrected him. "I'm looking for something better."

Seeing an opportunity, Dan said, "Maybe we should try somewhere else. In fact, I'm sure I saw one or two bookshops just now, and on the way, we can stop for a cup of coffee."

"Oh, I get it. This is about the fabled coffee shop you kept talking about. You couldn't find it, and now you want to drag me along to help you."

Is it that obvious? Dan managed a good-natured smile. "Something like that. I thought it would be...nice if we grabbed a coffee, but if you don't want to, that's fine. I can go ahead." He took a step back. "I'll see you later. Give me a call when you're ready for a lift. I can meet you at the car park."

"I've got a good mind just to let you go," Alan said. "I *can* tell you're bluffing, you know. I'm not a complete idiot."

Dan held up his hand in a conciliatory gesture. "I'll tell you what. Help me find the coffee shop and it'll be my treat. Anything you want."

Alan raised his eyebrows. "Why didn't you say that in the first place? Come on then. What are we waiting for?" Then without waiting for a response, he headed for the door.

Waiting? Dan thought. *Me? Never.* And he hurried after him.

***

Dan sat back, breathing in the coffee shop's steamy aroma. "You smell that? That's pure, mountain-grown Costa Rican."

"Yes," Alan said. "I love the smell of Arabica in the mornings. Smells to me like–"

"Victory," Dan interrupted. "Good try. You didn't get the quote totally right, but near enough."

"I was going to say *warm chocolate*," Alan protested. "And by the way, it's a bit rude to presume you know exactly what someone is about to say, especially if you're going to criticise them at the same time."

"But I often *do* know what people are about to say. And you're not a very good liar. You were going to say *victory*. You know it, and so do I."

Alan muttered something that sounded like, "Unbearable." But at that moment, a waiter arrived with a tray of steaming drinks, and the young man had, Dan noted with some satisfaction, a full beard complete with waxed-tip mustachio.

"Here we are, gents. Two large americanos. Special blend. And you didn't want any milk, is that right?"

"Well," Alan began, but Dan talked over him. "No thanks. We don't want to spoil it."

The waiter hovered, looking from Alan to Dan and back again, then he smiled. "Enjoy."

As he sauntered away, Alan glared after him. "He thinks we're a couple. I could tell."

Dan laughed. "What? But neither of us is gay. At least I'm not. And I saw the way you smiled at the young lady behind the counter. Anyway, it's ridiculous. We hardly know each other."

"You don't have to tell me that, but it's the way you insisted on me having the same drink as you, and...and..." Alan exhaled. "What's the use?" He took a sip of his coffee, and his expression brightened. "Actually, that's not half bad."

"You see. Always insist on the best."

"Even if you have to tramp around for half an hour to get it?"

"Even then." Dan took a long drink then set his cup down with a smile. "I'll buy some beans before we leave. Grind them back at the house." He paused. "And I'll have to buy a coffee grinder on the way to the car park."

"Hello again," someone said, and Dan turned in his seat to see the woman he'd encountered in the alley. "Did you find what you were looking for?"

"Yes," Dan replied. "Actually, we were looking for this place."

The woman laughed. She'd removed her coat, and she was dressed in an ivory cotton blouse over a pair of smart grey trousers. A single gold chain hung at her throat. "You should've said. This is my café." She looked around proudly. "A small place but mine own."

"But you said that there wasn't much down here," Dan replied. "*The best coffee shop in the city*, and you didn't think to mention it?"

Her eyes twinkled. "Well, I don't like to seem too pushy. People don't like it. And we're doing okay. Lots of regulars. Enough anyway. And some people come for the well."

"You have your own spring?" Alan asked. "Is that why the coffee's so good?"

The woman smiled. "No, we don't use the water. It's an ancient well. Come and have a look if you like. It's in the Roman room, at the back."

Alan practically jumped to his feet. "Yes, we'd like to see that, wouldn't we, Dan?"

Dan looked at his coffee. "In a minute, perhaps."

"Nonsense. We won't turn down this kind offer." Alan held out his hand to the woman. "I'm Alan, by the way, and this is Dan. He's from London."

"Ah, I won't hold it against him," the woman said, shaking Alan's hand. "I'm Deborah, but please, call me Deb." She looked expectantly at Dan. "Did you want to see the well? It's no problem if you don't. I'll leave you in peace."

Dan was about to snatch at the chance of a reprieve, but he caught Alan's glare and changed his mind. "Yes, thank you. It sounds...fascinating."

Apparently satisfied, Deb led Alan away, and Dan gulped down the rest of his coffee as fast as he could, doing his best to savour the taste. But the magic of that first sip was already lost. *I should just have said no*, he thought. *Why does everyone have to be so damned friendly all the time?* He cast a glance at the laminated menu standing proud in its stand at the centre of the table. Maybe he could order another cup in a minute, after this business with the well was concluded. *Who has a well in a cafe?* It sounded like a health and safety nightmare. But he pushed his chair back and trailed after Alan and Deb, making his way through an archway into the back of the café.

The room was small, snug and tastefully decorated in shades of cream and pale grey. There were a couple of worn leather sofas, but the rest of the space was taken up with tables and chairs. Except for the far-left corner. There, a set of low iron railings separated a quadrant of the cafe from something below floor level, though Dan couldn't quite make it out. Alan and Deb were standing at the railing, and he joined them, peering down. "Oh, it really is a well." He turned to Deb, studying her with frank curiosity. "Why?"

"This is our claim to fame," Deb replied. "Well, one of them, anyway. The ancient well of Saint Sidwell."

Dan held back a wry chuckle. The well was modern: a contrived affair of artfully placed stones with a plastic lining. Only a few inches deep, a layer of coins lay on the bottom, presumably tossed there by young children or other simple-minded individuals. Did Deb really think this was an ancient artefact? Surely not. She'd seemed to be quite a rational person–until now. "I see," he said carefully. "Not quite what I was expecting."

"Oh, this isn't the actual well," Deb said smoothly. "The original well was discovered a while ago, while we were having the floor re-laid. But we couldn't just leave a gaping hole in the corner, could we? We had to have it covered. But we built this to mark the spot."

"It's a legendary place," Alan put in. "Saint Sidwell was either Anglo-Saxon or she may have lived here around the time that the Romans were leaving Britain. And this is the place where she was killed. Murdered."

"You knew that already?" Dan asked Alan. "Is this a local legend that all Devonians know about, but no one else has ever heard of?"

"No, but I can read," Alan said, pointing to a sign affixed to the rear wall. "It's all there."

"Ah, yes." Dan pretended to read the notice, but his eyes soon wandered to the long shelves that ran around the room at head height. "Is that why you have all these...knick-knacks?"

"Ancient Roman relics," Deb explained. "They're reproduction, but the tourists like them. It gives the place a certain authenticity."

"While they sip their genuine Roman cappuccinos," Dan said with a smile. "I knew I should've worn my toga today, but it's at home in a vat of urine."

Deb laid her hand on her chest, and she stared at him in horror. "I'm sorry?"

"The Romans used it to bleach their clothes," Alan put in. "But don't worry about him. He's just being awkward."

"Right," Deb said uncertainly. "To tell you the truth, the artefacts all belonged to my great grandfather. He was quite the collector, and this place was his domain. The property has been in the family for generations, but he was the first to turn it into a shop."

"A real family business," Dan mused. "You come from a long line of proprietors. I'd have thought that would be authenticity enough."

"Maybe, but it wasn't always a café. My great grandfather was Gordon Kenning; you might have heard of him. He ran a number of pharmacies, but when he died, his son wasn't interested in taking over the business. The shop stood empty for a while. My father rented it out, but although lots of people tried to set up shop down here, they all failed. There isn't the footfall. No passing trade to speak of."

"But you're doing well," Alan said. "You must've turned it around."

Deb nodded. "There are quite a few big offices around here, and people will always venture out for a decent cup of coffee."

"Very true," Dan said with feeling. He gave Alan a meaningful look, but it was roundly ignored.

"What does the inscription signify?" Alan asked. "On the slab. Is that modern too?"

"Ah, now that is our little mystery," Deb said proudly. "That old slab of stone was hidden beneath the original floor, but it had been skimmed over with concrete. And when it was lifted, we found the well underneath. At the time, we had quite a bit of interest from historians and archaeologists, and they cleaned up the slab to reveal the carved message. It's not particularly old. It's probably Edwardian, but we're not sure exactly when it was put there, and no one knows what it means. It's all in code. It must be something to do with the well, so we mounted it there. It adds a bit of mystique, don't you think?"

Dan nodded firmly, his eyes bright. "Definitely." He licked his lips. "And you say no one has deciphered it, after all this time?"

"That's right," Deb replied, "though, to be fair, I'm not sure how interested the academics were. Once they found out that the stone wasn't an ancient relic, they weren't so keen. They finished their dig, took lots of photos, but they didn't find anything valuable. The next thing we knew, they'd all packed up and gone." Deb chuckled. "I had hoped to get the Time Team involved–the publicity would've been great for us–but they've stopped making it. Shame. Still, we got our room back and a write up in the local press, so it all worked out in the end."

"Tell me, Deb, would you mind if I take a crack at your cipher? Codes are kind of a hobby of mine."

"Be my guest," Deb said. "You'll have to copy it down though. You can't very well take the slab with you."

Dan pulled his phone from his pocket, leaning over the railings as far as he dared. "I'll take a photo. I should be able to zoom in from here."

Deb glanced over her shoulder. "I dare say you can pop inside. There's a gate I can open." She bustled along the fence and fussed over a combination lock before swinging a small gate outwards. "There you are. Proceed at your own risk, as they say. The rocks get a bit slippery, so don't go falling over and banging your head. My insurance people would go through the roof if they knew I was doing this."

"I'll only be a second," Dan said as he hurried in through the gate. Squatting beside the artificial well, he took several photos, checking they were sharp enough to read the garbled text, then he stood, pocketing his phone. "Got it."

Deb's indulgent smile gave him a moment's discomfort, and for a split second, he feared she might say, "Well done," as if he were a small boy mastering a mundane task. But as he rejoined Alan, his embarrassment passed, replaced by a different impulse. "Have we got time for another coffee, do you think?"

"Sure, if that's what you want," Alan replied. "You're driving today, so you're the boss."

"Right. Just a small one. An espresso perhaps."

"I'll put the order in for you," Deb said. "On the house. And I'll tell you what, if you can crack that code, I'll throw in a slice of chocolate cake next time you come in. And our cakes are *very* good."

"We'll see," Dan said modestly, and they headed back into the main room.

"I'd never have pegged you as a history buff," Alan said as they re-took their seats.

"I'm not. But I do like codes. I like the challenge."

Alan nodded. "I can tell."

"What do you mean?"

"Just that you seem...animated. Excited, even."

Dan grunted. "It's something to do. It'll probably turn out to be nothing. Just random graffiti or something."

"You're probably right," Alan agreed, "but you never know. Exeter is a very old city."

"So I gather," Dan said. And as the waiter appeared with a cup of espresso, Dan smiled. At last, a decent cup of coffee and a moment to enjoy it. The coded message was probably nothing. But this little cup with its perfect crema and its delicious aroma...*this* was something to get excited about.

***

"It's funny," Alan began as they headed back to the car, "but you'd think the old well would've been somewhere else entirely."

"Why's that?" Dan asked absently. "Originally, it must've been dug for a reason. There was probably a natural water source: a spring or something."

"Yes, but if we cut down that alley on our right, we'll be in the area that's actually called Sidwell, and it's nowhere near Deb's café."

Dan stopped walking. "What? That can't be right."

"I'm not making it up." Alan halted, gesturing to the open mouth of an uninviting side street. "Walk through there, and you'll find Sidwell Street, Saint Sidwell's School, Saint Sidwell's Community Centre. I could go on."

"But please don't." Dan set off again, taking long strides his gaze distant, and Alan hurried to catch up to him.

"So, that code...are you really interested in it?" Alan asked.

"Yes," Dan replied. "And I'm interested in something else too. I have a feeling that Deborah lied to us, and I want to know why. I want to find out the truth. And cracking that cipher is the first step."

CHAPTER 3

Embervale

Dan threw his pen down onto the kitchen table and ripped off the top sheet from his A4 pad, crumpling his scribbles into a ball and staring into space. "No, no, no." He should give up, take a break, but he picked up his pen once more and started carefully writing the letters of the alphabet down one side of the pad.

A knock on the front door interrupted his train of thought, but he ignored it. The only person he knew in the village was Alan, and he wouldn't be knocking on the door already, would he?

Another knock rang out, this time on the window behind him, and when Dan turned around, Alan was peering in. Apparently, the lack of response at the front door hadn't been enough to discourage him, so he'd made a swift circuit to the back. Was he always going to be so persistent?

"I wondered how you were getting on," Alan called out.

Dan shook his head and shouted, "Nothing yet. I'll talk to you tomorrow."

"What?" Alan cupped his hand to his ear.

"For God's sake." Dan jumped to his feet and went to open the back door. "Come in. I need a break, anyway. I've been staring at this thing for hours."

Alan smiled. "How about a cup of tea? I usually find that it helps when I'm tackling the crossword."

"Which one do you do?"

"The *Independent*. It's the only paper I can be bothered with these days. I do the quick one, then I tackle the cryptic."

Dan raised an eyebrow. "I'm impressed."

"I'm not just a pretty face, you know. I like to keep sharp."

"I'd have thought with your writing...all those stories. They must take a certain amount of mental effort."

"Kid's stuff," Alan replied. "Do you mind if I sit down?" Without waiting for a reply, he took a seat at the table and pulled the pad toward him. "Did you say something about tea?"

"No, but I'm guessing you'd like some. It's just a wild shot in the dark."

Alan sent him a smile. "Milk, no sugar. And if you don't mind, not too strong. The tannin sets my teeth on edge."

"I don't have any milk, but if you don't mind it black, I'll see what I can do." Dan gave the kettle an experimental swirl then filled it up at the sink. "Tea isn't really my thing. I don't know Earl Grey from Darjeeling." He rummaged through the contents of a wall cupboard and pulled out a familiar box. "I do know PG Tips though, so that's what you're getting."

"Fine," Alan said. "I prefer Yorkshire Tea myself, but I'm not fussy." He flicked through Dan's pages of unruly notes while, across the kitchen, spoons and crockery were industriously clunked together.

"There you go." Dan plonked a mug of tea on the table in front of him, the brown liquid almost overflowing, and Alan took a cautious sip.

"Thanks. That's very...full."

"No short measures here," Dan replied, taking a seat and regarding Alan for a moment. "If you're expecting me to have solved this already, I'll have to disappoint you."

"Not at all, I just fancied taking a look at it myself. You know how it is. You start thinking about a problem, and your mind won't let it go."

"Tell me about it." Dan let out a dry chuckle. "That's pretty much all I did, back in London. Solve problems. One after another."

"It sounds quite exciting, the life of a high-tech troubleshooter. It makes me think of the Wild West. The lone sheriff, riding into town, outwitting the locals and outshooting the bad guys."

Dan smiled. "You're not far off the mark. There were certainly plenty of showdowns, but they took place in air-condition boardrooms rather than dusty streets. And my weapons of choice were the Power-Point presentation and the frosty email."

"Pity."

"Yes. And ironically, I'm a pretty good shot. I was the top scorer at the corporate clay pigeon shoot."

"We have the real thing around here," Alan said. "Pheasants. Every Monday in the season. You should try it. I could introduce you to the chap who runs it."

"Thanks, but I don't suppose I'll be around all that long." He hesitated. "I have to get back to London at some point, I suppose."

Alan managed a smile. "It was just a thought." He took a slurp of tea. "If you're interested, I did a bit of research into the Saint Sidwell story."

"Me too. Tell me what you've got, and we'll compare notes."

"Sure." Alan sat up straight. "According to the legend, Saint Sidwell, also known as the patron saint of Exeter, was a beautiful young woman called Sativola, and like all young heroines, she was the kind and good-natured type. But her father was a rich man, so when her mother died, along came a stepmother, and of course, she decided to have the girl killed."

"Enter the grim reaper," Dan put in.

"Yes. There was a man who came to cut the long grass nearby, and the stepmother paid him to kill the poor girl, possibly while she was outside the city walls."

Dan nodded. "Interesting detail, that. The café we visited was well *within* the old walls."

"You have been doing your research," Alan said. "There are a few parts of the wall still standing. I could show you if you're interested."

"Maybe. In the meantime, google maps is a wonderful thing. But back to the story. The reaper took his money and duly chopped off young Sativola's head." It was Dan's turn to furrow his brow. "Damned tricky, I'd have thought."

"I don't know. A heavy, agricultural scythe in the hands of a skilled labourer, his muscles hardened by years of hard work."

"Even so," Dan said, "a certain amount of hacking must've been involved."

"This isn't CSI," Alan protested. "Legends are full of people cleaving each other in twain. But anyway, one way or another, poor Sativola was killed, and where she fell, a miraculous spring appeared. There are some references to her ghost standing on the spot, head under one arm and scythe in the other, but I don't think we need to go into that."

"Quite. My disbelief is suspended pretty much to its limits already."

"In that case, you definitely won't like the next bit. People drank from the spring, and their illnesses were cured, the lame walked, the blind could see, and so on."

Dan grunted under his breath, but Alan carried on. "The well was said to be a gift from God, and Sativola's name goes from Latin to English, becoming Sidwell. She's declared a saint, and a church was built dedicated to her name. It was bombed in World War II and had to be pulled down, but a new one was built, and it was later turned into the Community Centre."

"You've done a good job," Dan admitted. "You've found a few details I missed."

"All those years in the classroom. When you have to teach a topic to a room full of thirty kids, you need to get a grip on the subject pretty quickly."

"But you forgot the underground passages."

"I've taken the tour," Alan replied, "but I don't see what they've got to..." He frowned. "Ah, yes, I see what you're getting at. The passages were dug hundreds of years ago to take fresh water into the city. Did they run from Saint Sidwell's spring?"

"They did, indeed. So the locations of the various wells have been known for a long time. They're very much on the map."

Alan stared down at the table. "So you were right. Deborah lied about her well." He looked up. "But maybe she just made a mistake. She seemed like such a nice person."

"That's one heck of a big mistake. Most people, on finding a hole full of water under their floor, don't suddenly leap to the conclusion that it's something from an ancient myth. And if, as she claims, local historians visited the site, they must've told her that it was nothing to do with the saint, unless they were staggeringly inept. In fact, I'm surprised that the residents of Exeter aren't up in arms about it. Isn't the place teeming with retired colonels and schoolmasters: the kind of people who write long letters to *The Times* complaining about litter and the low moral fibre of the nation's youth?"

Alan laughed. "That's the problem with Londoners. They think everyone outside the M25 is some kind of character from a 1950s costume drama, but we have all kinds of people living and working in Devon, from bricklayers to orthopaedic surgeons and all points in-between. I've met quite a few folks who've come here specifically to escape from the city of your birth, and by all accounts, they enjoy the quality of life, the fresh air and the rolling hills. You won't admit it, but it's a nicer pace of life here. You've only been here a day, and I reckon you've got a bit of colour in your cheeks already."

"It's warm in here, that's all." Dan nodded toward the A4 pad. "Now we've agreed that the well is a fake, I ought to have another go at solving this damned cipher."

"Yes. Somehow, it doesn't fit with Deb's story. I suppose she's just trying to attract a few tourists. Certainly, her regular clients wouldn't be interested in her Roman bits and bobs. They'll dash in for their caffeine fixes and then be on their way, scuttling back to their offices."

Dan gasped. "Of course. That could be important."

"What? The local office types?"

"No. The Roman artefacts. She said that they'd belonged to her great grandfather. And the stone slab was Edwardian. Could the two have been contemporaneous?"

Alan tilted his head from side to side. "Edward the Seventh was 1901 to...to..."

"Come on, come on. What kind of teacher doesn't know this stuff?"

"I taught primary. The kids in my class were ten or eleven. King Edward did not feature heavily in our curriculum. The Victorians, on the other hand, were a big hit. Who doesn't love a ride on a steam train and a trip down a coal mine?"

"People with asthma?" Dan offered. "Anyone who suffers from claustrophobia?"

"Give me that pen," Alan growled, holding out his hand. Dan passed him the plastic biro, and Alan started writing, jotting down dates and then crossing them out. "Of course, we don't know how old Deb is. We can make a guess, but we also don't know how old her father was when she was born, nor how old her grandfather was when her father was born."

"I'd put her in her late forties," Dan said. "As for the rest, assume the parents were around twenty. Back then, people tended to have children earlier than they do now."

"I'd already thought of that. Hang on." Alan scribbled out a date and tried again. "Yes, I can make it so that her great grandfather was born around 1900, but I think Edward died in 1910. If this person was ten years old at the time, it's not likely that he'd go around carving messages into slabs."

Dan pulled a phone from his pocket. "Damn. I keep forgetting that there's no signal in here. And there's no router in this house. Can you believe it?"

Alan nodded, smiling. "Yes, but before you say anything, we are *not* in the Stone Age. This must be the only house in the village without reasonable broadband. You should have a word with your sister. She needs to get this place up to date. Most holiday cottages have wifi these days."

"I'll tell her the next time she deigns to phone. But somehow, I don't think that my lack of Internet is likely to bother her while she's swanning around San Francisco."

Alan took out his own phone. "I can just about get my wifi from here. What did you want to check?"

"The Edwardian dates. You didn't sound too confident."

Alan raised an eyebrow, but he began tapping on his phone's screen. "Yes, 1910. I thought so. But it does say this: *The period is sometimes extended in both directions to capture trends from the 1890s to the First World War.*" He lowered his phone. "I'm not sure how that helps."

"It helps because it puts the carving of the slab firmly in the same period as Deborah's Roman-obsessed great grandfather, yes?"

"I don't know about *firmly*, but I'd say we were on a steady wicket."

"I have no idea what that means," Dan said smoothly, "but let's take my theory and run with it. Can I take a look at your timeline?"

Alan pushed the pad towards him. "Bit messy. Sorry."

"Oh dear. Stay behind and copy it out a hundred times."

"Huh. I don't know what kind of school you went to, but that kind of inane punishment went out of fashion long ago."

"I attended a very expensive school. I won a scholarship. And to save you the time of jumping to conclusions, yes, it was riddled with ridiculous traditions and run by certifiable masters, most of them spicing up their lessons with psychological bullying and barely restrained violence."

"My God," Alan breathed. "Teachers like that should be locked up."

"Some of them have been. A good thing too." Dan smiled. "As you can see, though, I have emerged unscathed: a productive member of society. Until recently, anyway." He sat back, running his hands through his hair. "I don't know what I'm doing here, really. I only came on a whim, to take my mind off the hook, but here I am, mucking around with codes. It's displacement activity, I suppose."

"You're occupying yourself," Alan suggested. "Nothing wrong with that. Everyone needs a break now and then." He shifted awkwardly in his seat. "Listen, I know it's none of my business, but I think you came here for a reason. You wanted a change, but you're not the type to sit and do nothing. So, now that we've started on the puzzle, we may as well see it through to the end." He hesitated. "Do you have the original message written out?"

Dan sighed. "I did have it, but I threw it out...accidentally." He pulled out his phone and swiped the screen. "Here. We'll have to copy it out again."

"Thanks." Setting the phone down carefully, Alan began writing out the message, zooming in on the image to check each character. "Do I have to include all the dots? Are they punctuation or something?"

"I didn't bother with them," Dan replied. "I thought they were just there for the look of the thing, but then I didn't get anywhere, so maybe we should try keeping them in."

"Will do." Alan sat back to admire his work:

IO··NE·EE·B··SERNRCKGLBRNSYFOES.·YYE·OR··O·OFNS·M·RNAVOT-TOTL·S··EOIN·ETAONHLAEW·MFLIBDHKO·EY·LA·

"Not much to go on," Alan concluded. "Do you think the word spacing has been kept?"

"I thought so to begin with. But there are four letters that stand on their own, each different, and the only one-letter words I can think of are *I* and a."

22

Alan pursed his lips. "They could be digits. But let's backtrack a second. Why did you think the great grandfather's interest in the Romans was relevant?"

"Partly intuition," Dan replied, "and partly because I thought he might have used a Caesar cipher. It's a substitution cipher. Each character is represented by another."

"Yes. I made those once with a bunch of Year 5s. You shift the alphabet along a few places, so A becomes E, and B becomes F. Great fun."

"A codeword makes it harder to break," Dan said. "You pick a word that only uses each letter once. For instance, *Alan* is no good, but *Daniel* would work. You write down the codeword, then you fill in the rest of the alphabet, omitting the letters of the codeword."

Alan nodded. "So if I used *Daniel*, that would cover the first six letters of the alphabet, then I'd start with B, C, and...F?"

"That's right. It's better if the codeword uses at least one letter from later on in the alphabet, so *crazy* would be a good one. That way, you scramble the alphabet more thoroughly."

"Without the codeword, where would we start?"

Dan drummed his fingers on the table. "So far, I've been counting the numbers of letters and trying to work from there. That should help with a Caesar cipher because it's a straight substitution, and we know that in written English, *E* is the commonest letter, followed by *T, A, O,* and *I*."

"And in our message?" Alan asked.

"I wrote it down somewhere." Dan started picking through the crumpled sheets of paper scattered across the table. "Here it is. *O* and *E* are the commonest, then *N, S, R* and *L*." He tossed the paper over to Alan. "See what you can do."

For several minutes, Alan scribbled combinations of letters then tried to decode portions of the message. Dan watched, drinking the last of his tea and putting the empty mug in the sink. He stared out the window, lost in thought, taking himself back to the peculiar Roman room in the café. *Why does she bother?* he wondered. Would anyone really be taken in by Deborah's display of fake artefacts? Surely, the gleaming swords attached to the walls were obvious reproductions, as were the clay lamps and storage jars arrayed along the shelves. It was all just so much junk. Tacky. But then, perhaps that was what tourists wanted.

Wasn't London full of the same kind of nonsense? Model red buses that hadn't been seen on the streets for many years, Buckingham Palace snow globes, union jack baseball hats: it was all there. *We don't even play baseball*, he thought. *Where's the logic?*

Logic. The word nagged at him. There ought to be some logic to the placing of the carved message. If the connection wasn't the Roman trinkets, then what was it? *There's nothing else to go on*, he decided. *We have to assume it's got something to do with the Romans, otherwise, we've got nothing.* But he was missing something, something important, something he *knew* but he couldn't recall. What the hell was it?

His thoughts were derailed by the grating of Alan's chair as he pushed it back from the table. "I can't make it work. I'm getting nowhere. We need to try something else." He exhaled noisily and threw down the pen. "What about the simple one? The one where they wrapped it around a staff."

Dan stared at him. "My God, that's what I've been trying to remember. A scytale cipher." He sat down beside Alan, grabbing the pad and pen and running his finger along the coded characters. "Okay. Step one, there are ninety-six characters. Now we need to find all the factors of ninety-six."

Alan rubbed his hands together. "This is more like it. Mental maths is more my thing. So, one and ninety-six, two and forty-eight, three and thirty-two, obviously. Four and...let me see...twenty-four. Yes. Then six and sixteen. And of course, eight and twelve. Did you get all that?"

"Got it." Dan was already drawing rectangles on a fresh sheet of paper.

"I thought you needed to have the same diameter staff to decode it. Isn't that the way it works?"

Dan smiled. "Yes and no. A scytale is a transposition cipher. The letters are just jumbled, not replaced, and that's why none of our attempts have worked so far. But now, we just need to rearrange the letters into the right pattern, and we'll see the original message."

"Okay, but that could take ages, couldn't it?" Alan checked his watch. "I'm getting peckish."

"This won't take long." Dan paused. "To code the message, a strip of paper was wrapped around a staff, then the letters were written along the length of the staff, one on each turn of the strip, yes?"

Alan nodded. "That's the way we did it in my class. But surely, you at least need to know how many times you've wrapped the paper around the staff."

"It would help, but we can work around it. Picture what would happen if we ran a knife along the staff."

"Lots of little strips."

"Yes, and all the same length," Dan said. "If we laid those strips next to each other, they'd form a rectangle, and because there are ninety-six characters, and all the strips are the same length..."

"The sides of the rectangle must be factors of ninety-six," Alan said, grinning. "I wish I'd thought of that before. My class would've loved that. We could've had a competition to see who could crack a code first."

But Dan wasn't listening. He swept on, sketching out more rectangles as he spoke, dividing each one into hastily drawn grids. "We need a rectangle as a kind of matrix to write the message in. Any of the factors of ninety-six are possible for the lengths of the sides, but some are unlikely. For instance, it would be difficult to have thirty-two turns of the strip."

"I see what you mean. What if I take eight by twelve, and you work on six by sixteen?"

"Good idea," Dan said, ripping off a sheet of paper and thrusting it towards him. "I've already drawn them on there. Unfortunately, you'll have to try twelve by eight as well. We've no way of knowing which way around the rectangle will be."

"Okay." Alan studied the scruffy grids Dan had drawn. "Do I fill it in horizontally or—"

"Vertically," Dan interrupted, already filling in one of his own grids. "When you get to the bottom of one column, go to the top of the next one."

"Okay. And I suppose I'll soon be able to figure out if I've got the right rectangle."

Dan didn't look up. "The words will start to emerge. So if you're getting gobbledegook, stop."

They worked in silence for a minute, Alan craning his neck to read the coded message he'd copied out earlier. But suddenly, Dan placed his palms flat on the table, and he stared straight ahead.

"What is it?" Alan asked, his mouth dry. "What have you found?"

Dan's only reply was to point to the sheet of paper, and Alan took it from him. "In memory of Cyril Kenning," he read aloud, then he gasped, scanning through the rest of the decoded message. "My God," he whispered. "It's a gravestone."

CHAPTER 4

Exeter

It was almost lunchtime, but there were few customers in The Aquifer Café when Dan strode in with Alan following somewhat reluctantly at his heels.

At the counter, the young lady flashed him a smile. "Good morning. What can I get for you?"

"Just the owner, please," Dan said. "Deborah. If that's her real name."

"You want to see Deb? Er, are you a sales rep or something? Only, I can tell you that she's not interested in—"

"No," Dan interrupted, raising his voice. "I'm a dissatisfied customer."

The young lady paled. "I'm sorry. I'll...I'll see if she's available." She hesitated. "Can I offer you a drink while you wait? On the house, obviously."

"No, thank you."

"Oh. Right. Give me a second." The young lady hurried away, and Alan let out an exasperated sigh. "Did you have to do that?"

"What?"

"Make a fuss. None of this is the poor girl's fault. No need to take it out on her. She's probably a student or something, trying to earn a few quid to pay the bills."

"With her immaculate hairstyle?" Dan asked. "No. Students all look like they've just got out of bed...someone else's. They have that faraway look, like they're not sure where they're meant to be."

"Not in Exeter," Alan stated. "The university seems to attract a certain type. Their jeans are artfully ripped by skilled experts in the salons of Milan."

"Do they have salons in Milan? It's a French word."

27

Alan looked as though he was tempted to roll his eyes. "It was a joke, but never mind. She's coming."

Deborah breezed in, the young lady following behind and still looking worried. "Thank you, Camilla. I'll have a chat with these gentlemen. You go back to the counter." She flashed a warm smile at the young lady then turned a considerably cooler gaze on Dan. "Now, what can I do for you? I understand you have a complaint."

"Not really," Alan began, but Dan talked over him.

"Who was Cyril Kenning?"

Deb's expression froze, but a flash of uncertainty flickered in her eyes. "Gentlemen, if you have a genuine complaint, I would be grateful if you would say so. I'm happy to refund the cost of your purchase, but I don't have time for games. I'm a busy woman."

"Very impressive," Dan said. "But likewise, we don't have time to beat around the bush. You have Cyril Kenning's gravestone in the back of your shop, and I think you know perfectly well what it is. That raises a number of important questions, don't you agree?" Dan pulled a piece of paper from his pocket and held it out to her. "This, as you can see, is the message we decoded from the stone slab, so apart from a few answers, we're also entitled to the chocolate cake you promised, not that I really want it."

Deborah didn't even glance at the paper. "I think you've made a mistake. More than one, actually. Now, if you don't wish to order anything, I suggest that you leave quietly." She pulled herself up to her full height, raising a hand to point at the ceiling. "We have CCTV."

"So what?" Dan held her gaze. "We're not the ones in the wrong here, Deborah. You were quite happy for me to look at your fake well when you thought I was just another tourist from London."

"There's nothing fake about our well," Deborah shot back.

Dan chuckled. "Oh please. You must know that there's absolutely no connection between this place and Saint Sidwell. You're just trying to cash in on a local legend. But I don't care about that. It's the gravestone that concerns me."

"I believe that I've made myself clear. I have nothing more to add."

"You have to be kidding," Dan insisted, but Deborah raised her voice and snapped, "Out. Now!"

Dan took one look at the determined set of her jaw and knew he'd get no further. "All right. If that's the way you want it, we'll go, but I'm not done digging yet. I'll get to the bottom of this, with or without your help." He turned on his heel and stalked to the exit.

Alan hurried after him, answering the hostile stares of the other customers with an apologetic smile, and once the door had slammed shut behind them, the pair set off at a brisk pace, Dan with his hands thrust deep into his coat pockets. "Damn! You do realise what this means."

Alan nodded. "Yes. It means that you can't go back there ever again No more nice coffee."

"Exactly. I'll have to find somewhere else. But it won't be easy."

"You'll live." They walked on in silence for a while, then Alan added, "Did you mean that—about getting to the bottom of the story?"

"Of course. You said it yourself. Once you start on a problem, you want to finish it. So...you'll give me a hand, yes?"

Alan grinned. "My pleasure."

***

Back in the village, when Dan had bumped his battered Toyota over the uneven surface of his pitted drive, Alan paused before climbing out. "Do you want to use my Internet to do some research? It's no trouble."

"I thought you'd never ask. Is now a good time? Do you have space in your busy schedule?"

Alan nodded. "Would you be deterred if I said no?"

"Not really. I'd have turned up anyway, but I'd have brought biscuits or something."

"Is that what they teach you in the world of high-tech corporations? Productivity through bribery with buns?"

"Actually, yes," Dan said. "Doughnuts are good, muffins are okay, but if you really want results, a box of cupcakes works wonders. I find you can get people to do pretty much anything if you give them a dangerously large amount of frosting."

In Alan's kitchen, they sat at the large pine table, Dan fidgeting while Alan set up his laptop.

"Oops. Orange light. The battery's a bit low. I'll just go and fetch the charger."

"Could you log in first?" Dan asked. "I can get started while you hunt through your cables."

Alan raised an eyebrow. "I know exactly where my charger is at all times. It'll only take me a second to fetch it, but if you really can't wait, my password is H, w, g, g, n, i, m, w, i, n. The first H is uppercase."

"Interesting," Dan murmured as he typed in the sequence. "I'd bet that *win* stands for windows, and the rest is probably an acronym of some sort."

"I can neither confirm nor deny that statement," Alan replied, keeping his expression neutral, "and any attempt to steal my identity is a complete waste of time."

Dan looked up sharply. "Why? Is your cybersecurity bulletproof? Are you one of those paranoid people who refuse to use google? Do you spurn the pleasures of Facebook in an effort to prevent your every move from being tracked?"

"No, it's just that I haven't really got any secrets worth pinching. My life is...not dull exactly, but safe. Predictable. Fixed."

"Everyone has something worth stealing," Dan said. "Everyone."

Alan chuckled as if Dan had made a joke, then he headed into the neighbouring room, leaving the door open.

While the ancient laptop booted up, Dan let his eyes wander around the neat room. "Nice place you have here," he called out. "Not what I was expecting somehow, but I like it."

Alan reappeared in the doorway, holding out a charger, its cable neatly folded against the black plastic box and carefully secured with a rubber strap. "Here it is. It was exactly where it was meant to be. And...thanks. I like it in this room. I spend most of my time in here. It gets the light all year round." He paused. "But what did you mean about it not being what you expected?"

Dan shrugged. "Not your typical bachelor pad. No pizza boxes mouldering in dark corners. No piles of dirty crockery teetering in the sink."

"I keep the place tidy," Alan retorted. "I may be single, but I'm not twenty-one. This isn't...oh, what's that film? The one with Richard E. Grant and one of the McGanns?"

"Withnail and I."

"Yes. That's it. Great film." Alan unwrapped the charger's lead and plugged it in at the wall before sitting down and attaching the lead to the laptop. "That should do it."

"Thanks. To work." Dan opened a browser, then his fingers raced over the keys as he rattled through a number of search queries, his brow furrowing deeper as he rejected each set of results in favour of a fresh search. "I thought there'd be more results. Cyril Kenning isn't a particularly common name."

"But he lived in an age when nothing was digital. There'll be archives, but you often have to join one of the genealogy sites to get access."

Dan grimaced. "I don't want to get distracted by chasing down rabbit holes. We just need some reference to his war record."

"Pass me the decoded message," Alan said, and when Dan pulled the sheet of paper from his coat pocket, Alan laid it flat on the table.

In memory of Cyril Kenning a beloved brother taken too soon by the folly of a senseless war.

"We're assuming that it has to be the First World War," Alan began, "but could it have been another conflict? The Boer War? The Crimean?"

Dan pursed his lips. "Let me check. We guessed that Gordon was born at around the turn of the century, so assuming that Cyril really was his brother, we need to allow a few years either way for his date of birth, say 1897 to 1903. Okay, the Boer War happened at around the time Cyril came into the world. And the Crimean was even earlier. Let's stick with the Great War. If Cyril was Gordon's younger brother, he might've only been fifteen when the war finished, but if he was an older brother, he might have been twenty-one. He could easily have been involved in the fighting, couldn't he?"

"I would assume so. I believe that some people even lied about their age to enlist. Tragic for him to have died so young." Alan shook his head sadly. "Try searching for *roll of honour*. And add the term *Exeter* to narrow it down. After all, if his family were local business people, he may well have joined a local regiment."

"We don't know for sure when the pharmacy was set up, so we can't assume there's a link with the area, but I'll try it, anyway." Dan took just a second to complete the search. "I have the city's roll of honour, but I can't see a Kenning among them." He scrolled back through the list of names. "My God. So many."

"It makes you think," Alan agreed. "There can't have been many families who didn't lose a loved one."

"No sign of a Kenning though."

Alan sighed. "I'm starting to wonder if this isn't in poor taste. And anyway, it was all so long ago. Is it really worth dragging it all up?"

"I think so. There's something odd about that stone slab, and it's not just that it was in code. It doesn't belong in that café. It's been moved, and I want to know why." He looked Alan in the eye. "And there's Deborah's sudden change in attitude. Very strange, don't you think?"

"Not really. You did charge in like a bull at a gate. Has anyone ever told you that you tend to rub people up the wrong way?"

"Me? Certainly not. I'll admit I can be a bit...goal oriented, but I don't set out to offend anyone. Not usually, anyway." Dan sat back, his gaze growing distant. "When I showed Deborah the message, she didn't even look at it. It was as if she was denying its existence. She didn't want to know, and yet, when we first went in, she was happy for me to take photos of the code. She even opened the gate for me."

"She probably thought you'd post it on social media, spread the word about her café. As you said, she thought we were tourists. She wasn't expecting to see us again. Tourists are like sharks: they have to keep in motion, their mouths wide open, constantly consuming new experiences, or they stop enjoying themselves."

"Do sharks have a keen sense of fun, do you think?" Dan asked. "They always look dour to me."

"There's no need to pick holes in every metaphor I use. You know perfectly well what I mean, and my point stands. Deborah laid it on a bit thick when we were potential punters, but when you turned up in the role of the indignant dupe, she thought she'd be better off cutting her losses and kicking us out. Which, I might add, is a pain in the neck and all your fault. It's all right for you. You might not be sticking around, but I live here, and I would've liked the option of going back."

Dan jutted his jaw. "It wasn't entirely down to me; she was deliberately concealing something. And anyway, it wasn't your kind of place. You want organic oolong and chequered tablecloths, sugar tongs and china cups."

"I resent that," Alan snapped. "I'm not some middle-aged old duffer. I'm as trendy as the next man."

"Providing that the next man is dressed exclusively from Marks and Spencer's autumn catalogue." Dan raised his voice to match Alan's strident tone, adding, "and not last autumn either, but 2017."

The two men glared at each other for a second, but then a burst of laughter forced its way between Alan's tight lips. "2017! This shirt was already getting frayed around the cuffs by then. It's five years old if it's a day."

Dan joined in the laughter. "Sorry. I didn't mean to...you know."

"It's all right. It's been a while since I enjoyed a decent argument. That's one thing I miss about teaching: the cut and thrust."

"I thought you taught ten-year-olds. They can't have presented much of a challenge in a heated debate."

"Don't you believe it," Alan replied. "Children can be fiercely attached to their ideas, and they're often reluctant to change them unless presented with concrete evidence to the contrary." Alan paused, grinning. "Take this, for example. Two cups of ice, identical in every way. The same amount of ice in each. One cup is wrapped in a woolly jumper, the other left unwrapped. Which ice will melt first?"

"The unwrapped one, obviously. The wool will insulate the other one and protect it from the warm air in the room."

"Ah, but to a child, a woolly jumper is something that makes them hot, so almost all of them will predict that the wrapped ice will melt first."

Dan laughed. "I like it. There's a little bit of logic in there. I suppose we all interpret the world according to our experiences."

"Yes, and when it comes down to it, adults aren't much better. Hot air rises, right?"

"Yes," Dan said slowly. "I'd say so, even though I'm sure you're about to trick me in some way."

"No trick. Just a question. What provides the upward force?"

"Well, it's the current of air. Warm air is less dense, so it sort of floats upwards."

Alan smiled. "Almost there. But you still haven't answered my question. What force on Earth shoots things upwards into the sky? What provides this mystical upward push that you believe in so strongly?"

"I...I don't know." Dan frowned. "Go on then. Tell me the answer."

"The force involved is gravity, and it works in the opposite direction, pulling things towards the centre of the Earth. The denser, cold air is pulled down more strongly than the less-dense warm air, so it descends, displacing the warm air."

Dan's face fell. "My God. Why have I never thought of it like that?" He shot Alan an appraising look. "There's obviously more to teaching than I thought. Maybe you should've stuck to it. You obviously have the knack."

"Ah, I loved the job but not the way of life. Too much paperwork, too much government interference. It grinds you down, gets in the way. I still miss being in a classroom, but I don't envy today's teachers. Good luck to them."

"At any rate, while you were putting my brain cells through their paces, one or two things have shaken loose." Dan paused. "Did you do that on purpose?"

Alan folded his arms. "I couldn't possibly say. Trade secret."

"Okay. Well, we've been blinkered in our efforts to find Cyril. For one thing—and I can't believe I'd overlooked this—his family had a business in Exeter, but that doesn't mean they lived in the city. Deborah said that her great grandfather owned several pharmacies so the family could've been based elsewhere."

"Definitely. Let's look for the business and work back. Try searching for a pharmacist called Kenning."

"On it." Dan tapped the keys, and a smile lit his expression. "Got it. Gordon Kenning turned a single pharmacy into a whole chain of shops all over the country. It looks like he was a real entrepreneur, ahead of his time."

"What about Cyril?"

Dan shook his head. "Wait. I'll run a search on Gordon and see what we can find. Yes. Here he is. Cyril Kenning was Gordon's older brother."

"That must be our man. We could check the parish records or look for his grave," Alan said. "Any mention of where he lived? Is there a town, a village?"

"Better than that." Dan turned the laptop around to face Alan. "Behold, the ancestral home of the Kennings. Knightsbrook House. A crumbling manor house rebuilt on the proceeds of the pharmacy empire."

Alan leaned forward to study the screen, and his mouth fell open slightly. "But that's near here. It's just the other side of Bovey Tracey. It's less than ten miles away. I've seen the signs from the main road."

"And it's open to the public. We could swing by tomorrow, take the guided tour."

"Really?" Alan asked. "You want to go to that much trouble?"

"Sure. Anyway, you can't just buy a ticket and poke around. You have to take the tour, apparently."

Alan wrinkled his nose. "I don't know. I do have a book I'm supposed to be working on. I'm getting behind."

"Nonsense. The break from routine will make you work all the better when you get back to it. And look here." He pointed to the screen. "They have an excellent restaurant for visitors. Locally sourced ingredients. Pies, it says, are their speciality."

"Oh, well. Pies." Alan patted his stomach. "When do you want to set off?"

"They don't open until nine-thirty, so around nine?"

"Fine by me," Alan said. "Do we have to book the tour?"

"Just doing it now. I'll pay for the tickets, and we'll sort the money out later."

Alan nodded. "Fine. And I'll drive. I know the way, and it's down a narrow lane. You're probably not used to our little byways."

"If you can drive in London, you can drive anywhere."

"Even so, we'll take my car," Alan said. "It's my turn."

CHAPTER 5

Dartmoor

Sitting in the passenger seat of Alan's Volkswagen Golf, Dan clung to the door handle. "Mind that pothole. You can't get around it."

"Watch me." Slowing just a little, Alan sent the Golf veering across the narrow lane with a deft adjustment to the steering wheel. Twigs protruding from the high hedge lining the narrow lane scraped along the car's side, tapping on the window as the car flitted past. "There. Oops, there's another pothole."

"This is insane," Dan grumbled. "Are you sure this is a road? It's more like a track." He pointed through the windscreen. "It's got grass growing down the middle of it for God's sake."

"This is practically a motorway in Devon. No problem at all. Plenty of passing places."

"And we've stopped in most of them. For every mile forward, we must've reversed half a mile to let a Land Rover or a tractor to get past."

"That's nothing out of the ordinary," Alan replied. "You get used to it. And everybody gave us a friendly wave."

Dan stared out in silence. He wanted to ask how long it would take until they arrived, but he didn't want to sound like a petulant child. *Get used to this?* he thought. *No thank you. Give me traffic lights and bus lanes any day of the week.*

As if reading his mind, Alan said, "I'd rather be here than in a city. Once city dwellers get behind the wheel, they get rude and impatient. Here, we have to make allowances for each other, and most people are fine. You get the odd maniac, of course, but on the whole, it's a lot more relaxing than urban driving."

Dan wanted to contradict him, but he had other things on his mind, like watching the blind bends ahead and wondering what lay around them. Were they about to hurtle into a head-on collision with a combine harvester?

"Nearly there," Alan went on. "Just another minute."

"Great," Dan said, albeit without much conviction; they seemed miles from anywhere. But when they rounded the bend, the hedges fell away, the countryside opened up around them, and there, across a broad verge of neatly mown grass, a huge pair of wrought-iron gates stood wide open, a gravel path leading away between rows of evenly planted trees. And firmly fixed to one of the tall, stone gateposts was a dark blue sign with bold white lettering:

Welcome to Knightsbrook House.

They followed the signs to the visitor car park, and Alan brought the car to a halt in one of the many empty spaces.

"It's very quiet," Dan said, gazing out across the expanse of gravel. "I hope we got the dates right. It *is* open, isn't it?"

"The gates were open," Alan replied. "We're just a little early. For *some* reason."

Dan grunted. "I didn't want to miss the start of the tour. Anyway, we're here now, so let's go and have a look around."

A winding tarmac footpath took them through an area of landscaped garden, the path bordered with trimmed shrubs, and the route apparently designed to conceal the house from view until the last possible moment. But suddenly, there it was. Knightsbrook House stood proudly in its place, its walls of mellow stone pristine in the early morning light, its elegant proportions exuding an aura of permanence. Dan had always found mansion houses to be cold, pretentious even, but while this building was certainly grand, its rows of tall, leaded windows lent it a warm and welcoming aspect.

"Very nice," Alan murmured. "Talk about life goals..."

Dan smiled. "Yes, I can see you striding out with a shotgun over your arm and your faithful Labrador at your heels."

"Oh, I'd have half a dozen dogs if I lived in a place like this. A whole pack of them."

"Let's just hope they don't set the dogs on us today," Dan said. "I have a feeling we'd better watch our step. They won't like it if we seem too nosy."

"Agreed." Alan nodded toward the corner of the house where a grey-haired man in a dark jacket and trousers was bustling toward them. "This might be the butler coming to give us a horse-whipping."

"I've never been sure what that means. Do you have to use an actual horse-whip, or is it just an elegant term for sticking the boot in?"

But the man offered a friendly wave as he hurried toward them. "Hello," he called out. "You must be Mr Corrigan's party."

Dan and Alan shared a look. "Erm, there are only the two of us, I'm afraid," Alan said.

"So I see," the man replied with a smile. "You're our first guests of the day, and you're in good time which we do appreciate. It makes things difficult if people are running late." He paused to pull a sheet of paper from his pocket. "My name is Arthur, and I'll be taking you around the house this morning, but before we go on, do you have your ticket codes? There'll be an email if you booked online. Most people do it that way."

Dan fumbled for his phone, swiping his thumb up the screen. "Here we are." He held the phone out, and Arthur leaned close to peer at it before consulting his sheet of paper. "Thank you, that's all in order." He squared his shoulders. "Right, gentlemen, if you'll follow me, I'll show you inside. It's a little early, but unless you'd like a comfort break, we'll proceed with the tour."

Dan glanced around. "Don't we have to wait for the others?"

"Others?" Arthur studied him. "We seem to be at cross purposes. I understood that you were a party of two."

"We are," Dan replied. "I just thought there would be other people joining the tour."

Arthur shook his head. "No, sir. Just the two of you. It's early in the season. We do have much larger groups in the summer, but today, you have my undivided attention, so if you have any questions, please feel free to ask as I show you around. But let's head over to the entrance hall, and I'll begin." He extended his arm toward an imposing front door and then led the way, striding purposefully, his back straight, and Dan and Alan fell in behind him.

"I feel like I'm on a school trip," Dan murmured to Alan.

"Sh," Alan replied. "No talking in the ranks."

Dan grinned, but the sensation of being a schoolboy on a class outing did not disperse as they were led from room to room, gazing appreciatively at paintings as Arthur recounted the tales of the people portrayed. And despite his courteous manner, Arthur was clearly a man on a mission. He whisked them from place to place, maintaining the flow of his oratory until one impressive room blurred into another.

Finally, when they reached a spacious conservatory, Arthur relaxed a little, and standing in the centre of the room, he favoured them with a beatific smile. "Now, gentlemen, we're almost at the end of our time together. We have one more room, and then you'll be free to explore the gardens at your leisure. So if you have any questions, this is a perfect time to ask them."

"Yes," Dan began, "you've told us a lot about Gordon Kenning and his heirs, but there's been no mention of Cyril."

Arthur raised his eyebrows. "Goodness me, you have done your homework. I've been a guide here for fifteen years, and no one has ever asked about Cyril Kenning."

Dan narrowed his eyes, but before he could speak, Alan said, "We're very keen on local history, and we came across a reference online."

"I see." Arthur nodded thoughtfully. "I'm sure you know that Cyril was Gordon's older brother, but I'm afraid that there isn't much more to tell." He smiled, but Dan detected a hint of sadness in the man's eyes. "You must appreciate that this house, while impressive, is still a family home and not a museum. That's why we run these tours instead of letting people just wander around. The family are entitled to their privacy, and we must respect their wishes, wouldn't you agree?"

"Yes, but Cyril died a long time ago, in the First World War, wasn't it?"

There was a pause before Arthur replied. "Like so many, Cyril served and was lost. And like so many, he was only a very young man when he died." His professional smile and brisk manner were back. "If there are no other questions, I'll take you through to the final room, and since you're interested in the Great War, you'll enjoy it. Follow me, please."

He set off toward an unmarked door, and Alan followed, but Dan stayed behind for a moment, gazing around the tidy conservatory. *Not a museum*, he thought, but somehow, he couldn't square that statement with his impression of the place. The house, in all its glory, seemed stuck in the past, frozen in time. If a young man with carefully oiled hair and wearing a striped blazer were to saunter in through the French windows twirling a tennis racquet, he wouldn't be surprised.

"Come on, Dan," Alan called out, and with weary feet, Dan traipsed after him.

In the next room, Arthur was waiting, his hands clasped in front of him, and Dan was immediately struck by the profusion of objects displayed in the glass cases that lined the room. Undoubtedly, this *was* a museum.

"There has been a long tradition of government and military service in the Kenning family, and indeed, the current owner of Knightsbrook House, Martin Kenning, served with the Royal Marines, rising to the rank of major. When he retired, he decided to put the family's collection of uniforms, military paraphernalia and other artefacts on display, so he had this modern extension built. Everything is arranged in chronological order and clearly labelled, so I'll give you a while to peruse them as you see fit. Then, when you're ready, I'll show you out to the gardens and direct you to our Orangery Restaurant for any refreshments you might require."

"Thank you," Alan said, then he crossed to the first display case and leant close to study the scarlet dress uniform within, clearly intent on reading every word of the caption below.

But Dan paced the length of the room, scanning the artefacts rapidly.

Arthur cleared his throat. "Is there anything I can help you with, sir? If you wanted the First World War items, you've just passed them. They're behind you on your left."

"I'm looking for a Roman general's staff," Dan said, his eyes roving across the displays. "It'll be a reproduction, a replica, but I feel as though it'll be here."

"No, sir. I know every item in this room, and I can provide a good amount of detail on most of them, but these artefacts all date from 1830. Many of them predate the house, of course, but thankfully, the family were very good at maintaining the older items in good order. Now, the dress uniform that's occupying your friend is—"

"Not really of interest to me," Dan interrupted. "Where is it? The staff. He used it for the scytale, but where is it now? Does Deborah have it?"

Arthur eyed Dan warily. "Sir, I presume that you are referring to the Roman reproductions collected by Gordon Kenning, yes?"

"Yes. Can I see them? They weren't in the house. I checked as we went around, but there was no sign of them."

"That's because the collection is private," Arthur replied. "None of the items are displayed since the family felt that they would cause confusion or give an impression that could've been...misleading."

Dan stared at him. "Misleading? In what way?"

"Well, as you have already surmised, most of the items were reproductions and of no real historical value, but in a house such as this, visitors might've assumed that they were genuine. The family were keen to avoid that situation."

Alan joined them. "Sounds very reasonable. People are fast to jump to conclusions, and then they feel foolish or cheated when they find out they're wrong."

"Precisely, sir," Arthur said. "There were a few genuine artefacts in the collection—pottery fragments and so on—but they were either sold or donated to the Royal Albert Memorial Museum in Exeter. As for the rest, they were packed away several years ago and placed in a storage facility."

Dan nodded thoughtfully. "I see. Okay, in that case, is there anything here that belonged to Cyril Kenning?"

Arthur blinked as if taken aback at the sudden change in topic, but he recovered quickly, his expression becoming stern and fixed. Remaining tight-lipped, he shook his head.

"Nothing?" Dan asked. "Nothing at all? Even though he served in the War?"

"There are no items relating to Cyril Kenning in this room, sir." Arthur took a breath. "Mr Corrigan, I really don't know where you're going with this, but please remember that the artefacts around you have all been kindly provided by the Kenning family, and they are entitled to choose what goes on show to the public." He let out a humourless chuckle. "After all, if I were to visit your home, I wouldn't expect to go rifling through your photograph albums."

"I don't have photo albums," Dan replied, "I don't even have photos. Nobody has photos anymore. But the point is, I don't sell tickets to my front room and charge people for the privilege of staring at my over-stuffed sofa."

A flush of colour tinged Arthur's cheeks. "Sir, I have nothing further to add, so if you'd like to make your way through the exit, you'll find the Orangery Restaurant around to your right. It's clearly signposted." He sidestepped to an unmarked door and pulled it open, gesturing toward the doorway. "Please feel free to explore the gardens, sticking to the marked paths in order to preserve the lawns. Thank you for visiting Knightsbrook House, and I hope that you've enjoyed your tour."

"Hold on a minute," Dan began, but Alan intervened.

"Thank you, Arthur, you've been very helpful, but..." Alan glanced back at one of the displays, "I hate to tell you this, but you're not quite right."

"I beg your pardon, sir?"

Alan pointed to a uniform tunic displayed on a stand. "That was Gordon Kenning's uniform, yes?"

Arthur nodded enthusiastically as if relieved to be back on familiar territory. "Yes, sir. Third Battalion, Devonshire Regiment. They were a Special Reserve unit, but they did important work, training officers and men to equip them for the challenges they'd undoubtedly face."

"Yes, I read the caption," Alan said. "But that ribbon...if I'm not mistaken, that represents the Croix de Guerre 1914 to 1918."

"How do you know that?" Dan asked. "I didn't have you down as an armchair general."

"I'm not, but I knew we were coming here today, and I did my research. Most of this collection is listed on the website, and the medal caught my eye. It seemed strange to me that a British soldier could be awarded such an important French honour, so I looked it up."

"Well done, sir." Arthur beamed. "As I'm sure you discovered, units of the British Army and other allies of the French could be awarded the Croix de Guerre for their gallantry, in this case, for the defence of Bois des Buttes in May of 1918."

"Yes, I found that out online, but it doesn't tally with your display." Alan fixed the man with a searching look. "You see, if the person who wore this uniform belonged to a reserve unit, how could he have been recognized for his gallantry in a battle? I'm sure the third battalion played their part, but from what you've just said, they weren't frontline troops. The Croix de Guerre was awarded to the second battalion, most of whom were killed in the fighting."

Arthur's smile faltered. "I'd have to check the precise details, sir, but there's no question about the medal's authenticity, I can guarantee that. The family would never allow such a thing. As I said earlier, the current owner was an officer in the Royal Marines."

Alan held up his hands. "Oh, I'm sure the medal is genuine. I just don't think it was awarded to Gordon. I think it was given to someone else, probably Cyril."

"I think we're onto something," Dan said, taking a step closer to Arthur. "What happened to Cyril Kenning? And why has he been airbrushed out of your little museum?"

Arthur bristled. "Sir, I've done my best to answer your questions, but I believe that I've made the position clear. I have nothing more to add, so that concludes the tour. As I said, you may visit the restaurant and the gardens if you wish. Thank you and goodbye." He stood stiffly beside the door, stony-faced, and after a brief moment, Dan turned to Alan. "Come on. We may as well go."

They headed outside, and the door was closed firmly behind them.

"Tell me," Alan began, "if I hang around with you, am I going to be continually thrown out of places?"

"Very probably," Dan replied. "If you play your cards right." He smiled. "Good work with the medal, by the way. You weren't bragging when you said you were good at research."

Alan affected a nonchalant expression. "One tries." He pointed to a wooden signpost. "I think we've earned a trip to the restaurant, don't you?"

"I guess we could have an early lunch. I don't suppose they'll have much I can eat, but they must be able to rustle up a snack."

"Are you allergic to gluten or something?"

"I'm a vegan. Sort of."

Alan's gaze shot skyward. "It's such a fad. Everyone's doing it these days. But how can you be *sort of* vegan? You're either a vegan or you're not."

"I eat fish, but I'm damned if I'll use the word *pescatarian*. I won't bore you with my objections to meat and dairy products, but fish...frankly, they've got it coming."

"Wait a minute," Alan protested. "You didn't say anything about all this when I mentioned the pheasant shoot."

Dan sighed. "I don't bang on about my principles every five minutes. It's not like I'm a member of some weird cult or religion. I make my choices, you make yours. I won't pour scorn on you if you buy a meat pie, nor will I make rude remarks while you eat it. À chacun son whatsit."

"Goût," Alan provided. "Okay, let's go and see if we can find a mung bean you can nibble."

"As I said, I won't cast aspersions on your lifestyle, so I'd be grateful if you'd return the favour." Dan looked him in the eye. "As far as I'm concerned, this is not a fad but a choice, and I made it a long time ago. It's got nothing whatsoever to do with Gwyneth Paltrow or any of the other so-called celebrities. It hasn't always been easy, but I've put a lot of thought into my decisions and I stand by them. I think that deserves a little respect."

Alan dipped his chin. "Fair point. No more snide remarks. And for the record, I'm with you on the fish. I've always found them to be fundamentally untrustworthy."

"And that is a sentence I never thought I'd hear," Dan said. "Come on, let's get to the restaurant before Arthur calls out the guard."

"He's probably looking for a horse-whip as we speak," Alan said with a smile, and they set off along the gravel path.

CHAPTER 6

Knightsbrook House

After lunch, they strolled into the grounds, following the meandering path between carefully tended flowerbeds.

"Admit it," Dan said. "That pie was good."

Alan nodded. "Chestnut mushrooms in red wine with a hint of thyme. Who knew?"

"The chef, it would seem. Ah well, if nothing else, we've had a good lunch."

"More than that," Alan replied. "We've had a useful trip. But we couldn't really talk in the restaurant. The lady behind the counter was hanging on our every word."

"Bored, I expect. The place was deserted." Dan threw him a sidelong glance. "What did you want to talk about?"

"Cyril's medal, of course. We must be able to work something out. There can't have been too many Croix de Guerres handed out to British soldiers. And Arthur seemed very certain of the specifics, so the battle he mentioned might well be the right one. I'd guess that there must've been a citation of some kind, but whether the name was changed by accident or design, we don't know. Still, all we have to do is look up the battle and we might get one step nearer to finding Cyril Kenning."

"Possibly," Dan conceded, "but it's pretty thin. All kinds of mix-ups can happen in a war. Gordon might've been deployed at the last minute, or perhaps he was caught up in the action unexpectedly. I suspect that Arthur doesn't know the truth, so he covered up his lack of knowledge with bluster. It happens."

"I suppose so." Alan halted, his hand pressed against his stomach. "Do you mind if I sit down for a minute? I wolfed that lunch down a bit too quickly."

Dan eyed him suspiciously. "If you're going to have a dig at vegan food, may I remind you that you could've chosen anything from the menu? Nobody asked you to come out in sympathy."

"No, I'm being serious. I usually have a light lunch. You know, just a quick sandwich." He pointed across the path. "There's a bench over there. We could sit down and make a plan, decide where to go next."

Dan raised an eyebrow. "You want to carry on? Do you think we'll get anywhere?"

"Yes. Actually, I'm getting more intrigued as we go along. I really feel like there's an interesting story behind all this. It might even be something I could write up."

"I don't think your readers would like it," Dan said. "What's the average age of your fans, nine or ten?"

Alan waved his objections aside. "No, no. This would be for adults. I could use a pen name. People do it all the time."

"All right, let's figure out what to do, but we'll keep walking if you don't mind. I think better when I'm moving. And anyway, we'd better stay on the path, or we might have Arthur chasing after us."

They followed the path, strolling past pristine lawns and threading their way between rose beds laid out with geometrical precision and miniature hedgerows of neatly trimmed box. For a minute or two, Dan enjoyed the peace. He could actually smell the flowers, even though they were just beginning to burst out from their buds. Not the choking dust of diesel fumes, not the acrid tang of car exhaust, nor the lingering spicy aromas of Asian restaurants, but actual flowers: blooms that looked as though they'd been planted generations ago and tended carefully ever since. And he could hear birds singing from the trees up ahead. Not pigeons squabbling and cooing, but songbirds celebrating the arrival of summer. He listened, but he couldn't hear a single car. Not one. No aeroplanes either. He took a deep breath, filling his lungs. Even the air seemed sweet, and maybe, just maybe, this whole countryside thing wasn't so bad after all.

"I don't know why I've never been here before," Alan said, breaking the silence. "I suppose you tend not to appreciate what's on your own doorstep."

"Very true. Back in London, there's so much to see, but like most people, I hurry past most of it on my way somewhere else."

"That's no way to live," Alan stated. "It's no wonder everyone's suddenly so keen on going to mindfulness classes."

Dan nodded. "Somebody suggested that I should try it when I...when I felt unwell." He risked a furtive glance at Alan. Had he said too much?

But Alan was looking around as they walked, his face turned upward to feel the sun's warmth. "And did you? Try the mindfulness, I mean."

"No. There was a three-month waiting list." Dan smiled. "I don't think I could've stood it, anyway. Not my idea of fun."

"Well, you know what they say about meditation," Alan replied, "it's better than sitting around doing nothing."

Dan laughed. "I must remember that. Maybe I can have it printed on a mug."

"I'm here all week. Don't forget to tip your waitress."

"Speaking of which," Dan began, "maybe we should make another visit to a certain coffee shop in Exeter."

Alan looked doubtful. "We're not exactly flavour of the month in The Aquifer Café. I don't think Deborah will talk to us, and confronting her again would be a mistake."

"You're probably right. We could look online for the battle Arthur mentioned. What was it again?"

"Bois de something," Alan replied. "I remember the date though. May 1918. And we have the regiment. I'd take a look on my phone, but I'm hardly getting a signal out here. It'll be easier at home."

"Okay, but what can we do *now?* You mentioned graveyards before. Presumably, there's a plain English gravestone for Cyril somewhere. Perhaps the coded message was originally alongside it. Where's the nearest church?"

Alan thought for a moment. "Bovey Tracey, probably, but it might not be the right one. Sometimes, wealthy families have a historical connection with a particular church."

"A family plot. Maybe even a mausoleum." Dan stopped walking. "Could Cyril's grave be here? On the estate?"

"Yes, I suppose so. There was no mention of a mausoleum on the website or in the brochure, but maybe they wanted to keep visitors away."

Dan rummaged in his jacket pocket, pulling out a crumpled leaflet and unfolding it eagerly. "I picked this up when we were on the tour.

Yes. I'll bet there's something interesting here." He held the leaflet out to Alan, jabbing his finger at the simplified map of the estate. "That whole area is marked as private. It has to be worth a look."

"You really are intent on getting us into trouble, aren't you," Alan said. "Ah well, in for a penny, in for a pound. Which way is it from here?"

"That way." Dan pointed across an area of open grassland. "If we go straight across, we'll be visible from the house, but we could run for it. It's quiet here today, so if no one's looking, we'll probably get away with it."

"I'm not twelve," Alan protested. "I'm not going to go dashing hell for leather through the middle of the estate. It'll look suspicious. Someone might call the police, and what will we say? *It seemed like a good idea at the time, officer.*"

"We *could* skirt around the grass, but that will take a lot longer," Dan countered. "And since we'll be breaking the rules anyway, the more time we spend off the marked path, the more chance there is that we'll be spotted. We might run into a gardener or a gamekeeper. But if we sprint over there, we'll be out of sight in seconds."

"Seconds! When was the last time you ran anywhere?"

"About eight days ago," Dan shot back. "Five K. I go three times a week, usually. I've missed a few recently for one reason or another. I need to get back into training."

Alan's face fell. "You never said you were a runner. In the pub, I got the impression you hated sport."

"No, it's games I don't like. I've been running for years. And I lift too. Free weights." He looked Alan up and down. "I take it you're a stranger to the gym, but listen, you'll be all right. It won't take long to jog across the grass; it's only a few hundred metres. You can manage it at a push, can't you?"

"Of course, I can. I just...I don't think it's..." Alan looked out over the expanse of grass, his gaze flitting to the house and back again. "Oh, sod it! It's no use arguing. Let's do it." And he set off at a brisk jog, his arms pumping stiffly, his elbows tucked tight against his body, and a determined set to his jaw.

Without hesitation, Dan hared after him, passing him easily, and he led the way to a clump of tall trees, weaving between the trunks until

he came to a clearing. There, he turned around, grinning and straightening his jacket, barely out of breath, watching Alan as he lumbered
closer, his cheeks puffing out, and a sheen of sweat coating his brow.

"Bloody hell!" Alan grumbled, staggering to a halt and clutching his
side. "I knew I wasn't fit, but that...that was horrible."

"We can stay here for a minute while you get your breath back. We
can't be seen from the house."

"Thank God for that." Alan threw back his head and gasped for fresh
air, then he stared at Dan. "And you go running for fun? For a hobby?
Unbelievable."

"You get used to it. It takes a week or two before you start to enjoy
it." Dan hesitated. "While I'm around, I could take you along on a run
if you want. Just until you get the hang of it. I need to get started again,
and I could take it easy, keep the pace low."

Alan let out a long breath. "Not heading straight back to London,
then?"

"I might stay. For a while."

"Okay." Alan stretched the word out, then he nodded as if reaching
a decision. "I can't believe I'm saying this, but you're on. I've got an old
pair of trainers kicking around somewhere. I suppose that's all I'd
need."

"Plus a pair of shorts. And we'd have to find somewhere flat for your
first time."

"Well, that's easier said than done when you live halfway up the side
of a valley," Alan replied. "There's always Tottiford reservoir. There's a
nice path, and I've seen other people running up there. There's only one
problem..."

"What's that?"

"No defibrillator for miles," Alan said with a grin. "Do you know
CPR?"

Dan chuckled. "Not really, but you'll be fine. Running is great for
your heart unless..." His smile faded. "You haven't got a heart problem,
have you? Hell's teeth, I should've asked."

"No." Alan puffed out his chest. "I have the heart of a twenty-year-
old. That's what the doctor said when I had my last checkup."

"In that case, we'll start tomorrow. Eight O'clock?"

"In the morning?" Alan asked. "What about breakfast?"

"Skip it. Just have some water and a piece of toast or something. Otherwise, you'll regret it."

"Too late," Alan moaned. "That ship has sailed."

"You can't back out now," Dan said. "Shall we move on?" He pointed across the clearing to a wrought-iron gate set in a low stone wall. "That looks like our way in. Are you ready?"

Alan nodded, then they made their way quietly through the clearing, scanning the trees as they went. The gate had no lock, but its hinges were thick with rust, and it groaned as Dan lifted the catch and pushed it open.

On the other side of the wall, the grass had been mown, the evergreen shrubs kept under control, but wildflowers had sprouted here and there, primroses scattered among the grass. Around the edges of the lawn, bluebells nodded in the breeze, and a rambling rose crept its way along the wall. The place evoked the genteel atmosphere of a forgotten cottage garden, as if it had always been there and always would be.

"A secret garden," Alan murmured. "Like something out of a child's picture book."

"I'll take your word for it," Dan said. "It doesn't seem like the kind of place you'd find a gravestone though. Maybe we jumped to too many conclusions."

"Perhaps, but we're here now, so we may as well take a look around." He gestured toward a barely visible gravel path that wound its way across the lawn before finally disappearing from view between a pair of tall shrubs. "Looks promising."

Dan nodded doubtfully, and they set off, marching along the path, gravel crunching underfoot. Neither man spoke, and as they walked, a sense of calm settled on Dan's mind. *Alan was right*, he thought. *This place is like something from a fairy tale.* Bees bumbled gently among the flowers or buzzed lazily through the warm air, small birds flitted from one shrub to the next, and the scent of freshly cut grass, pleasantly pungent, drifted on the breeze.

"It's nice, isn't it?" Alan said after a while. "Restful."

"Yes. I wonder why they don't open it to the public."

"Hm. The expense, probably. They'd have to maintain it, put up signs and so on. And then there's all the health and safety nonsense." Alan tutted under his breath. "It's a shame."

"I think there's more to it than that," Dan said. "They clearly don't want people walking around down here. There must be some significance to the place."

"You could be right, but before we go any further, I'm going to sit down on that bench for a minute." Without waiting for a reply, Alan struck out toward an ancient wooden bench, and Dan followed, dragging his feet.

"Ouch!" Alan winced as he sat down. "I think I might've pulled a muscle when I sprinted over the lawn. I'm having second thoughts about your kind offer to take me for a run in the morning."

Dan sat beside him. "Oh no. You can't give up before you've even started. I expect you've just strained a ligament a bit. Nothing a stretch and a hot bath can't cure. I'll make sure you warm up properly, tomorrow. You'll be..." His voice trailed away, and Alan cast him a questioning look.

"I'll be what? Dead on my feet? Out for the count?"

But Dan stared over his shoulder, and simply said, "Look."

Alan shifted in his seat to study the stone wall behind the bench. At first, he didn't react, but then he saw what had grabbed Dan's attention. "Oh."

Dan pointed to the wall, his finger tracing an imaginary rectangle. "That recess. It's exactly the same size and shape as the stone slab in Deborah's café."

"I can't say I'm one hundred percent positive," Alan said, "but you could easily be right. Check it against the photo."

"Of course." Dan grabbed his phone from his pocket, swiping the screen then holding it up to take an image of the wall before checking his photos. "Yes. That looks like a perfect match." He turned his phone around to show the screen to Alan. "Look at the proportions."

"So what about Deborah's story? She said they dug the stone up when they found the well."

"I'd guess that she invented the whole thing," Dan said. "She wanted to create a certain atmosphere, so she took the slab and made up a story to lend it some weight."

Alan grunted in disapproval. "Some people will stop at nothing for a bit of notoriety. That message was intended as a memorial stone for Cyril, and the bench too, I expect."

"Yes." Dan ran his eyes along the seat's back. "There's no plaque, but then, they wouldn't have needed one. They had the stone."

"So long as you knew what the coded message meant."

Dan ran his hands through his hair. "That's what's weird. Cyril was a war hero, so why hide his memorial away in this corner? Why not have it up at the house in pride of place? And why was there no mention of him in the museum?"

"Perhaps there was some cloud over him," Alan offered. "A family's reputation would've been important back then. There was something they wanted to hide."

"Maybe, but it's a funny way of going about it." Dan sat back. "On the other hand, communication must've been difficult in 1918, so maybe there was some confusion over what had actually happened to Cyril."

"This is just speculation. We need more information." Alan cocked his head to one side. "Did you hear that?"

"What?" Dan asked, but even as he spoke, he picked up the sound of a dog barking. "Yes. And I don't know much about dogs, but it sounds angry. And quite big."

"Definitely. And it's getting closer." Alan stood, looking around the garden. "I don't think we'll find out anything else. Time for us to go."

Dan nodded, standing up and brushing down the seat of his trousers. "That bench was getting damp, anyway. Ready for another run?"

"A brisk walk will be much better," Alan replied. "We'll attract less attention, and anyway, best not to tempt fate. Most dogs love a good chase." He set off along the path, taking long strides, and after a brief glance at the place where the stone slab had once been laid, Dan followed him towards the gate.

CHAPTER 7

Bovey Tracey

They said little during the drive back to Embervale, and for his part, Dan had no wish to discuss their departure from Knightsbrook House. As a grown man, he'd rarely been scolded, and to be dressed down by a groundsman and threatened with prosecution, all the while being fixed in the hungry gaze of an outlandishly large German shepherd, was a humiliation that he was keen to forget.

But when their route took them through the small Dartmoor town of Bovey Tracey, Dan sat upright in his seat. "This was the place you mentioned. The nearest church."

"Yes," Alan replied, his gaze fixed firmly on the road ahead.

"Well, maybe we could stop by the church, visit the graveyard. Or is there a cemetery?"

Alan let out a sigh of frustration. "Yes, there is a cemetery and a nice little church, but do you really expect me to take you there after what we've just been through?"

"It wasn't so bad."

"*Wasn't so bad!* I've never felt so embarrassed in my entire life. I've lived in this area for years; I have friends, acquaintances, people who know me. They know I'm a writer, and they know I was a teacher. How will it look if this gets out? And it probably will. A lot of people around here are connected."

Dan let out a dismissive chortle. "You make it sound like they're in the mafia."

"No, I mean that they're related or close friends. In these small towns and villages, people actually talk to their neighbours."

"Talk *about* them, you mean," Dan shot back. "Gossip—the last refuge of the small-minded. There's nothing else to talk about, I suppose."

A growl rumbled in Alan's throat. "You are being deliberately insufferable. You know perfectly well what I mean, and don't forget, we were the ones in the wrong. We were trespassing on private property."

"Debatable," Dan said. "There were no signs telling us to keep out, and we'd been told we could explore the grounds. I don't think the police would've been interested."

"That's not the point." Alan paused for breath, and when he spoke again, his voice was calmer, his tone more patient. "I have a reputation in the local community, and I don't want to get sly looks and stupid remarks every time I return a library book. Do you understand that?"

Dan hesitated before replying. "Yes. I can see that. And for what it's worth, I'm sorry. It was my idea to go into that garden, and I probably pressured you into it." He paused. "Why do I feel like I've just been lectured to?"

"Years of practice," Alan said with a wry smile. "Old habits die hard." He paused, his expression softening. "Anyway, there's no need to apologise. I made my own decision to go nosing around at Knightsbrook, and I'll have to accept the consequences. I'm just frustrated by the whole thing."

"So, does that mean you don't want to go to the church?"

"Well, we could drive home that way. If we go through the town, we'll get to the church, then there's a lane that'll take us straight to the cemetery."

Dan grinned. "Excellent. I would've come back on my own, but with two of us, it'll be much quicker."

"And more fun," Alan offered.

"Definitely."

They were able to park directly opposite the Church, and as they opened the gate to the churchyard, Dan read the sign. "The Church of St. Peter, St. Paul *and* St. Thomas. Isn't that hedging your bets?"

"Heathen," Alan said, following him onto the stone steps that led toward the church.

"No offence intended. Are you a regular churchgoer?"

Alan shook his head firmly. "No, I just like to show respect for people's firmly held beliefs, that's all. It's called tolerance. You should try it."

"I tolerate all kinds of things, but I won't bow my head to a wrathful God I don't believe in. Why should I? Where's the consistency in that?"

Alan's gaze rolled skywards, but he made no reply, and they trudged in silence to the nearest row of graves.

"I'll take this row, you take the next one," Dan began, then he turned with a start.

Across the churchyard, an elderly man rose stiffly from his knees beside a grave, a blue cloth in his hand. He was grey-haired, perhaps in his seventies. His craggy features were emphasised by the wrinkles in his brow, and he was smartly dressed in a tweed jacket and a pair of dark brown corduroy trousers. His expression was sombre, and he seemed surprised to have been disturbed, blinking as he stared at them.

"I'm sorry," Dan said quickly. "We didn't mean to intrude."

"That's all right," the man said, his voice mournful but not unkind. "I was just keeping the headstone clean. It gets algae on it otherwise. It's the rain."

"Of course," Alan said. "We'll leave you in peace."

"No, no, you carry on," the man said. "I was just leaving, anyway." He pulled a plastic bag from his jacket pocket, stuffed the cloth inside, and with a fond glance back at the gravestone, he walked away without a word, his back straight and his head erect.

Dan watched him go, waiting until he was out of sight. "I never thought about anyone else being here," he said. "I just assumed the place would be empty."

Alan shot him a meaningful look. "Let's make a start, but we'll go quietly. And don't go treading all over the graves."

"That goes without saying," Dan replied. "I'll start here. Are you happy to take the second row?"

Alan nodded, then they began their slow journey across the churchyard, picking their way carefully between the graves, and occasionally stopping to read an inscription from a headstone.

Dan's first pass yielded nothing useful, and since Alan was still strolling casually along the second row, he went ahead to the third row and headed back towards their starting place. *This is starting to get to me*, he decided. Reading the names of the dead, one after the other, and calculating their ages, his mind wandered to a dark place: the unvisited region of his consciousness where death and decrepitude lay in wait, and the remaining days of his life were measured out, second by second.

His gaze lost its focus, and he began skipping over the names, searching only for the date of poor Cyril's demise: 1918. But suddenly, he stopped. *What was the name on that last stone?* He retraced his steps, staring down at the simple headstone of dark polished slate, and there it was.

"Alan," he called out, trying to keep his voice from becoming too loud. "Come and see this."

Alan hurried to join him. "Have you found him? Is it Cyril?"

"No." Dan pointed to the headstone, an edge of excitement creeping into his voice. "But I have found a couple of family members. And from Knightsbrook, too. We saw a painting of Gerald, didn't we?"

"Yes. A portrait." Alan rubbed his chin as he read the rest of the inscription aloud, "In memory of Helen Kenning, a wonderful wife and mother, died 12th September 2005. And Gerald Kenning died 15th November 2005. A devoted son and husband, and a loving father." He nodded thoughtfully. "It looks as though Gerald died of a broken heart, barely two months after his wife passed away. You hear of it happening all the time."

Dan didn't reply. Thoughts of his own parents crowded his mind. He should call them. They'd be worried about him, wondering why he'd taken himself off from his home, his friends, his commitments. *I'll call later*, he told himself. *When I know what my plans are.* Then he pushed the thought away. He had no idea how long he intended to stay in Devon, and no idea what he was going to do next. None. And in the meantime, Alan was staring at him. "What?"

"Nothing. It's just that you look a bit..." Alan waved his hand in the air. "Listen, if you want to go home—"

"I'm fine," Dan interrupted. He forced a smile. "Okay, so you were the one hanging on Arthur's every word. What can you remember about Gerald?"

"Not a great deal. He was Gordon Kenning's son, and he inherited Knightsbrook House. He ran the pharmacy chain for a while, but I got the impression that he didn't have his father's entrepreneurial flair. After a while, he sold the business and lived off the profits."

"Very good," Dan said. "We're getting closer to the elusive Cyril. And there's something else. Look at the stone. It's spotless."

"It's certainly more recent than most of the others in this part of the churchyard."

"True, and that's why I almost walked straight past it, but that's not the point. This was the stone that the elderly man was cleaning. Look, you can see where he was kneeling on the grass."

Alan's mouth hung open a little. "No. Do really you think he was one of the Kenning family?"

"Absolutely. He must've been...let me see, Deborah's father. What was his name?"

"David," Alan replied. "Arthur mentioned him on the tour, but from the way he talked, I thought that David had passed away. He certainly doesn't live at Knightsbrook. The owner's name is Martin: Deborah's brother."

"I expect it's a full-time job running an estate that size. If that man really was David, he was certainly a pensioner. He would've retired some time ago." Dan looked over toward the gate, but of course, the man was nowhere in sight. "It's a damned shame. We could have asked him some questions."

"No, we could not. The man was tending to a grave, paying his respects. How could you even suggest such a thing?"

Dan held up his hands. "I wouldn't have hounded the poor man, I just thought...we could've talked."

"He had a lucky escape. You have all the tact of a gently lobbed hand grenade." Alan returned his attention to the headstone, sighing gently. "It's sad, isn't it? Even though we never knew them, it still gets to you." He sniffed, looking up. "It's the fact that they died in living memory; it makes it seem real. The graves from a hundred years ago are interesting, but this one is different. It must be one of the newest graves in the place."

"Yes. It seems a little out of place somehow. I wonder why he was buried here and not in the cemetery."

"Maybe he was involved with the church," Alan offered. "And the family were well known. It couldn't hurt to have been the owner of Knightsbrook."

"Is that how it works? Give generously, turn up every Sunday, and you're in?"

Alan shot him a pained look. "Cynic. For all you know, the Kennings were pillars of the community. Give someone the benefit of the doubt for once."

"Hm." Dan looked away, scanning the neat rows of graves that they'd yet to explore. Alan's down-to-earth pronouncements took some getting used to. In Dan's world, friends smiled and joked and bought rounds of over-priced drinks, all the while seething with jealousy and resentment, waiting eagerly for others to make mistakes, always an eye to the main chance. Cynicism and mistrust had always been essential; was there another way to treat people? A gentler, better way to live?

"Whatever the reason," Alan went on, "this could be the family connection we were hoping for. We should keep searching. Cyril might be nearby."

"Agreed," Dan said, and they returned to the hunt. But when they reached the final gravestone, over an hour later, they'd found no other graves of the Kenning family.

"The cemetery?" Alan asked, and Dan nodded.

"The cemetery."

It was a short journey to the cemetery by car, but as they turned in through the stone pillars of the gateway, Dan's heart sank. The rows of graves stretched out into the distance, and a thorough search would clearly take hours.

"I'll park here," Alan said, halting the car on a narrow strip of tarmac just inside the entrance.

"Is it worth it?" Dan asked. "We haven't got all..." But he let his sentence go unfinished, because there, striding toward them along the path, was a familiar figure.

Alan followed his gaze and let out a gasp. "Is that...? My God, yes, it's him. David Kenning."

"I know. But what do we do?"

"Nothing. Leave him in peace. And don't stare." Alan rummaged through the contents of the pocket in the door beside him, pulling out a tattered map and unfolding it. "Here. Look at this. Pretend we're lost."

Dan stared at him. "Seriously? You want me to *pretend*?"

Alan nodded. "So, if we take this road, there's no telling when we might get home because this is a road map of..." He checked the front cover. "Belgium. Thought so. Have you ever been?"

"Do I look like the kind of person who might've been to Belgium?"

Alan smiled. "Yes, actually. You'd fit right in. It's a lot more cosmopolitan than most people give it credit for."

"I have no idea what you're talking about, but meanwhile, David is right in front of us. If we don't talk to him now, he'll get away, and we'll lose him again."

"Good," Alan said firmly, keeping his eyes on the map. "I must go on holiday again soon. I fancy Berlin."

Dan didn't say a word. David Kenning was marching ever closer, his dogged strides bringing him directly toward the car, and for some reason, Dan couldn't look away.

David Kenning's senses were clearly undiminished, and his bright eyes flitted from Dan to Alan and back again, a frown furrowing his brow.

Dan fought the urge to wave, but when David was level with the car, he fidgeted in his seat, unfastening his safety belt.

"Don't even think about it," Alan muttered. "Let him go."

"But—" Dan started, but Alan didn't let him speak.

"You are *not* going to pester an old man, and anyway, there's no need to upset him. We can see which row he came from. It'll save us time."

Dan's shoulders slumped, but he didn't argue. He tilted his head until he could see David in the wing mirror, and he watched him make his way out of the gate. "He's gone. Come on." He opened the door and stepped out, waiting while Alan climbed out and locked the door. "Is that necessary?"

"Habit," Alan answered, making a show of trying the door. "Now, I first spotted David over there by that crooked white stone. We can start there."

"Yes," Dan said, leading the way, walking quickly.

Alan kept pace, and a moment later, they were studying the stones. "Here!" Alan cried out, pointing to a squat slab of white marble. "I've found Gordon."

Dan leaned forward to read the inscription. "In memory of Gordon Kenning, died 3rd February 1972 and Diana Kenning, died 10th March

1983. We are returning by the road we came." He straightened his back. "No mention of Cyril though."

"I don't know. There's something about that quote. I remember it from somewhere, and it doesn't seem right."

"How do you mean?"

"I'll look it up," Alan said, reaching for his phone. "I usually get a reasonable signal in town."

Dan blinked, looking out across the fields and hedgerows that surrounded the cemetery. "You call this *in town?*"

"Bovey Tracey is a fully fledged town," Alan replied without looking up from his phone. "It has a mayor and everything. Ah! Here it is. That line is from a poem by Siegfried Sassoon."

"The war poet."

"Yes; one of them. But here's the thing. The title of the poem is *To My Brother.*"

"Odd thing to write on a stone shared by a husband and wife," Dan mused. "We don't know if he chose it himself. His wife might've added it, or maybe someone else who just happened to like the sentiment of the words."

Alan frowned. "I'd be surprised if a woman were to choose that particular poem. It goes on:

Your lot is with the ghosts of soldiers dead,
And I am in the field where men must fight."

He pocketed his phone. "It's the kind of poem a soldier might choose. Sassoon wrote it on the death of his own brother who was killed in action, and I can't help thinking it was Gordon's way of making a reference to Cyril."

"Okay, but does it take us any further forward? Why would Gordon refer to his brother in such an obscure way? Epitaphs are usually definitive, aren't they? *Here I am. I was born, I lived, I died. End of story.*"

"For the most part, but I think Gordon must have been an odd character. Larger than life. An entrepreneur, an obsessive collector, a writer of coded messages. It's an odd mixture of traits when you think about it."

"Wealth does strange things to people," Dan muttered. "It rarely turns out well."

"I'll have to take your word for that," Alan replied with a smile. "I don't expect to strike it rich any day soon, thank goodness. But what do you want to do now? Shall we keep looking for Cyril?" He paused, turning around. "He might be in here somewhere."

"Worth a try," Dan said. "We'll split up again, but we need to move faster this time. No dawdling. Meet me back here in half an hour."

"Are you accusing me of dawdling?"

"Yes," Dan stated, "but don't take it personally. *Everyone* in a hundred-mile radius is determined to move at a snail's pace. It's a wonder anything gets done at all."

Alan grunted. "It's a little thing we have around here called quality of life. You might be wise to give it a go. Rush around all you want, but sooner or later, we're all going to end up like the residents of this place. You may as well enjoy the journey."

"Thanks for that *thought for the day*, but I like to get things done and move on. What's wrong with that? It's the way my mind works, and I'm happy as I am."

Alan looked him in the eye. "And yet, here you are. Why is that, Dan? You don't seem to like it much in this part of the world, so what are you doing here? Are you avoiding something?"

"I..." Dan exhaled noisily. He didn't have to tell Alan anything. Not one word. But there was something reassuring in the way Alan was looking at him, and suddenly, he found himself talking. "All right. If you really must know, I needed a break. I'd been working hard, dealing with a new client: Vortigern Finance. You won't have heard of them— not many people have—but they're a huge company, rolling out commercial software to some of the biggest businesses on the planet. I should never have taken the job on, but I thought I could handle it. Then things started to go awry. The CEO was accused of false reporting and kicked off the board, and it turned out that he'd been inflating the company's profits for months. They were in trouble, and the shareholders were howling for blood. Some projects were cancelled and there were redundancies, but I was a contractor so I would've been all right, except..."

"Go on," Alan prompted. "You may as well tell me."

Dan let out a humourless laugh. "It seemed like I was one of the lucky ones. I was taken on to help with the task of corporate restructuring. I really thought I'd landed on my feet—permanent contract, company car—but I was walking into a minefield. There were too many managers and not enough jobs, so they all clambered over each other, desperate to grab a slice of the action, all hungry for power. You don't know what these people are like. They'll do anything to further their own ambitions. Anything. And there I was, stuck in the middle." He held out his arms then let them flop to his sides. "I couldn't hack it. I worked night and day, tried every trick in my arsenal, but in the end, I crashed and burned. I couldn't deal with it anymore. I was a physical wreck, and mentally, I...well, I'd been used to calling the shots under pressure, with millions of pounds hanging on my decisions, but I woke up one day and I couldn't even work out what to have for breakfast. I was a mess."

Alan's hand went to his mouth. "I'm so sorry. What happened?"

"When you're working at that level, and in that kind of environment, you can't call in sick during a major upheaval and hope to get away with it. I took a couple of days and tried to pull myself together, but when I went back to work, I couldn't get past the front desk. They took my security pass and my laptop, then they marched me out of the building. And when I got home, there were a couple of goons waiting to take possession of my car. It was a BMW, a brand new X7, but it was a company car, and Vortigern wanted the situation made very clear. I was finished."

Alan ran a hand through his hair. "Bloody hell. They shouldn't have treated you like that. Surely, you had your rights, a contract."

"None of that mattered. It was better for me to walk away quietly. They knew it, and so did I. And when they took my car, it was the last straw. I had to get away, to disconnect. I phoned my sister to borrow that wreck of a Toyota, and she suggested I use her holiday cottage, told me it was empty while she was trying to get it refurbished. The rest, you already know."

For a long second, Alan stared at him, then he plunged his hands into his pockets and said, "You know what? It's time for a tea break. Let's go home."

"What about Cyril? We were going to search for him."

Alan shook his head. "I don't think he's even here. Think about it. Why would there be a message about Cyril on Gordon's headstone if the genuine article was close at hand? The line from the poem, the coded message from the garden, they're the act of a man trying to get something off his chest. For some reason, Gordon was denied the satisfaction of erecting an official headstone to Cyril, so he vented his grief elsewhere, and he did it quietly, making veiled references that other people wouldn't understand."

"Why?"

"That, I don't know, but with one thing and another, I don't want to hang around in this place for a second longer than is strictly necessary. So take a picture of the stone if you want to, then we'll head back to the car. We can talk about all this later, or tomorrow." He sent Dan a smile. "You know, when I'm working on a book, if I get stuck on the plot, I set the whole thing aside and go and do something else. I take a long walk or something, and it gives my ideas time to percolate. By the time I'm ready to start work again, the solution is usually ready and waiting for me."

"You could be right. I certainly feel like there's something obvious that we keep missing." Dan nodded thoughtfully. "I'm starting to wonder if we were right to let David Kenning slip through our fingers. He probably would've told us everything we needed to know, and then the whole thing would've been wrapped up." He smiled. "But I keep telling myself that the old boy doesn't owe us anything, and so, on balance...you were right. I'm glad we didn't bother him; he might've been upset, and that would've been awful."

"Good Lord," Alan breathed. "There's hope for you yet."

"Oh, I do hope not," Dan said, turning away from the grave. "I don't suppose you happen to have any cake lying around at your house, do you? I could murder a chocolate brownie."

"No, I'm afraid not." Alan patted his stomach. "I don't keep that kind of thing in the house. I need to watch my waist, and if I had a cake, I'd eat the lot in an afternoon and then regret it." He frowned. "Anyway, cakes are crammed with butter, aren't they? They'd be no good to you."

"You can make them dairy-free," Dan protested. "I know a recipe you can make in a mug. You just mix flour, cocoa powder, sugar and vegetable oil in a big mug, and then bung it in the microwave. Takes two minutes."

"Well, I've got a microwave, and we might be able to rustle up the rest. If you fancy a go, you're welcome to brave my kitchen cupboards."

"Deal," Dan said, his spirits lifting. But as they strode back towards the car, his step faltered.

There was no mistaking the figure who stood beside the car, his arms folded and his expression stern: David Kenning. And he wasn't alone.

CHAPTER 8

Bovey Tracey

The man standing beside David Kenning was perhaps in his early fifties, but although he was dressed in the kind of casual hiking clothes that bristled brand names, he somehow managed to look as though he was in full uniform and preparing to inspect the troops. He remained perfectly still, his arms by his side, but he radiated a sense of restrained energy, and he was staring at Dan and Alan with ill-concealed anger.

Dan found his pace slowing as he approached the two men. He'd faced down plenty of boardroom bullies in his time, but here, walking on grass rather than commercial-grade carpet, and surrounded by gravestones, he felt exposed, out of his depth. He glanced at Alan, searching for a cue, and perhaps his uncertainty showed because Alan said, "Maybe you should let me do the talking. I'll try to explain the situation."

But Dan shook his head. "Somehow, I don't think he wants explanations, and he looks like a man who'll be infuriated by excuses."

"He's certainly not happy," Alan muttered. "What's your plan then?"

"At a guess, I'd say he wants to get something off his chest. It might be better to let him get on with it. I know that look in his eye."

"Okay," Alan replied doubtfully. "But be polite. Don't antagonise him."

"We'll see." Dan lifted his chin and returned the man's stare. "Hello," he called out. "Can we help you with something?"

"I might say the same thing to you," the man said, his tone austere. "I'm Kenning, Martin Kenning, and I take it that you two are the *gentlemen* who visited my house this morning and harassed a member of my staff."

This was the opening salvo, a marker thrown down, but although Dan's heart began to beat a little faster, there was no way he was going to tuck his tail between his legs like a whipped dog. No. His spirits stirred, a cool surge of confidence washing over him, and Dan knew that the setting may be different, but this was *his* arena, and all he needed to do was keep his cool and trust his instincts. *I can do this*, he told himself, and for the first time in a while, he felt like himself. Perhaps it was the effect of unburdening himself to Alan a few minutes earlier, but Dan felt stronger, ready to slip into his professional persona, the familiar air of self-assurance wrapping around him like a well-cut suit. He wore his most unflappable smile, and he strode close to Martin, his hand extended for a shake. "Daniel Corrigan and this is my associate, Alan Hargreaves."

Martin cast an appraising glance over both men before shaking their hands in turn, but he did not return their smiles. Instead, he turned to David. "Okay, Dad, I'll take it from here. There's no sense in you standing around getting cold. Why don't you wait for me in the car?"

David Kenning squared his shoulders and looked ready to argue, but before he could say anything, Martin patted him on the arm. "It's all right, Dad. We'll soon have this straightened out. I'm sure that these gentlemen will listen to reason." Martin looked at them for confirmation, and Dan nodded with a reassuring smile.

"All right," David said, "but listen, what's this all about? Why the devil are you following me around? Are you journalists or something?"

"Nothing like that," Dan said quickly. "We were just—"

"Poking your noses in," David interrupted. "Well don't. There's no sense in dragging up the past. What's done is done. It was a long time ago. Let it lie. Let the dead rest in peace."

Alan shifted his feet, and he looked as though he was about to make a grovelling apology, so Dan spoke quickly, making his voice firm but unthreatening. "I can assure you, Mr Kenning, that we mean no offence. Our interest is purely academic. A personal project."

David screwed up his mouth as though he'd like to say more but couldn't quite bring himself to utter the words.

"Seriously, Dad," Martin said, "please go back to the car. I'll be along in a minute."

"Hm. Well, don't keep me waiting." David turned on his heel and marched away.

Martin watched him go, concern in his eyes, and when he turned to Dan, some of his anger seemed to have dissipated. "Well, you certainly know how to put the cat among the pigeons. I've had Arthur on the phone, telling me that you went wandering around and upsetting the gardener. And just the day before, my dear sister called me up, practically in hysterics. She was wittering on about two men who came asking questions, and that has to be you two, yes?"

Dan nodded. "We met Deborah in her café, and to be fair, she showed us the message on the stone slab. She was more than happy for us to try deciphering it."

"I see." Martin raised an eyebrow. "And what did you make of it?"

"Don't you know?" Alan asked.

"No. And I've never really thought about it. It was some old piece of nonsense. Gordon's probably. He was a bit of a crank. All kinds of gear in the attic. Most it got shipped off to the museum. Deb wanted the Roman knick-knacks for her little coffee shop, and I was glad to see the back of them."

"But, the stone slab was in the private garden, wasn't it? In the wall behind the bench."

"Yes," Martin replied. "And now I know why the gardener was upset. No one is supposed to go down there, not yet, anyway. It's not up to scratch. We had to have the wall fixed up before the damned thing fell down, and the carved piece was loose. It would've cost a lot more to have it cleaned and set back in its place, so when Deb asked if she could have it, I was all in favour." He paused. "So, what does it say?"

"It was a memorial to Cyril," Dan said, his hand sliding into his pocket. "I have the text here."

"No need," Alan put in. "I know it by heart. It said, *In memory of Cyril Kenning a beloved brother taken too soon by the folly of a senseless war.*"

Martin's face fell. "Good Lord. All these years and I never knew. We all assumed it was some sort of motto. *Carpe diem*, or some such." He shook his head sadly. "Poor old Cyril. A sad story. Well, I suppose I'll have to sort all this out and smooth down Deb's feathers. Damned nuisance, but it can't be helped." He let out a weary sigh. "It's a bit misleading, the message, but I expect you knew that already."

Dan frowned. "How do you mean?"

"Cyril of course. He wasn't killed in action. Far from it. The Great War was over when he died. 1919 if I remember correctly."

"That explains why we couldn't find him on a roll of honour," Dan said. "But why does the message say he was taken by the folly of war?"

Martin hesitated. "Cyril was my great grandfather's older brother, and by all accounts, they were close. Inseparable. The boys lost their father at an early age; Gordon was only five years old. So when Cyril died, my great grandfather was bereft and bitter. I can't say why he blamed the War. Maybe he thought Cyril was never the same after everything he'd been through. But I do know that Gordon turned his back on the military, the church, and even his own class. We're an old family, and we've been at the Knightsbrook estate for hundreds of years, but Gordon went his own way. He turned to commerce, and much to everyone's surprise, he was damned good at it. He made his fortune, knocked down most of the old manor house and had the present place built. After that, he became something of a recluse."

"He married though," Alan said.

"Oh, yes. They say that my great grandmother ran the estate. A formidable woman. Ahead of her time."

"We found her headstone," Alan began, "but..." Alan left his sentence unfinished, his lips clamped shut as if he'd said too much.

"What?" Martin asked. "What do you *think* you've found out? Come on."

"I'm not sure how you'll feel about this," Alan replied, "but the quote on your great parents' headstone might not be dedicated to either of them. You see, it's from a poem called *To My Brother*."

"I didn't know that." Martin lifted his chin. "Can't say that it makes much difference."

"It suggests that Gordon never forgot his brother," Dan said. "I hope you don't mind me asking this, but where exactly is Cyril buried?"

Martin's gruff manner was back, and he squared his shoulders. "He's not here. Don't waste your time."

"Where is he then?" Dan asked. "We'd like to see this through, if just for the sake of completeness, and we're keen to know what happened to Cyril."

"And what would you do with that information?"

Dan held out his hands, his palms upward. "Nothing. As I said earlier, we're not reporters. This is purely a personal project."

"No websites or blogs or social media?" Martin said the words as though they left a bitter taste in his mouth. "Nothing of that sort?"

Alan shook his head. "Nothing you tell us will be made public in any way."

Martin took a breath, his nostrils flaring. "It's very simple. From what I know, Cyril spent time in an isolation hospital in France. The War was over, but there was a massive outbreak of Spanish flu."

"A pandemic," Alan put in. "It killed millions around the world. There were more fatalities than the war."

Martin gave a curt nod as though that ended the matter.

"Where was the hospital?" Dan asked. "It's always nice to have the details."

"Calais," Martin said. "And that's all I have to say. There was no glory in it, and my father wants it forgotten. I bring him here to tend to the graves, and to the church too, but he served his time in the forces, as have I, and we don't dwell on Gordon's antics. My great grandfather had some pretty unpopular opinions in his day, and we don't want the family embarrassed. I hope that's understood."

"Yes," Alan said quickly. "I suppose that's why Gordon wrote his message in code; he didn't want his anti-war sentiments to be widely known."

"There's such a thing as survivor's guilt," Dan added. "Gordon was in a reserve unit, so I doubt whether he saw any action. Maybe he felt that he should've fought alongside his brother."

Martin stiffened. "I heard that you queried the authenticity of the Croix de Guerre, and I'll admit that a mistake was made. Arthur is a good man, and he means well. He knows his kings and queens, but he isn't a military man, and he doesn't appreciate the importance of the details. The uniform and the medal belonged to Cyril, but my father didn't want Cyril's name displayed, and I bowed to his wishes. Gordon's uniform is identical except for the insignia, and it's displayed alongside

69

Cyril's. The caption must've been moved by accident. A minor slip up and easily corrected. I'll see to it myself."

"I see," Alan said. "Thank you for straightening that out."

"Glad to be able to set the record straight," Martin replied. "I hope that this draws the matter to a close."

Dan nodded, but he remained tight-lipped.

Alan cast him an inquiring glance, then he turned his attention back to Martin. "Please assure your father that our researches have reached an end. I hope we haven't caused him any offence."

"He'll get over it," Martin said, extending his hand for a shake. "It's a good thing that we ran into you. Best to get these things sorted out."

"Yes," Dan said, shaking his hand.

"Thanks for your help," Alan added as he took his turn to shake hands.

"Right, I must be off," Martin said, and turning on his heel, he marched away.

"Who'd have thought?" Alan mused. "We go for a coffee and end up talking to a retired major about Spanish flu. What are the chances of that?"

"Virtually nil," Dan said. "But there's just one problem."

Alan furrowed his brow. "What?"

"He was lying. His story doesn't add up."

"You can't know that," Alan argued. "It all sounded plausible to me."

"The best lies often do," Dan said. "But if this is just about the Spanish flu, why did David assume we were journalists? Why was Martin so concerned about whether we'd be publishing the details online?"

"The family's reputation—"

"Nonsense," Dan interrupted. "They're trying to cover something up, and I want to know what that is."

"But I told him we'd stop."

"Yes, but I didn't agree to that," Dan countered. "I want to go on, and despite himself, Martin gave us the next clue."

Alan hesitated, thinking. "The isolation hospital in Calais."

"Exactly. Martin doesn't have the imagination to make up something like that, but I'm willing to bet he hasn't told us the whole story."

"I think you might be right," Alan admitted. "His stiff upper lip routine was a bit over the top. After all, a soldier dying from an illness is nothing to be ashamed of."

"Exactly," Dan said. "And we're going to uncover the truth."

CHAPTER 9

Exeter

Dan turned around on the spot, gazing up at the glazed roof of the Royal Albert Memorial Museum, taking in the sweep of the grand staircase, the curve of the archways perched atop the polished pillars. "Not bad," he murmured. "Not bad at all."

"I'd forgotten how nice it is," Alan said. "I should visit more often."

Dan raised an eyebrow. "*Nice?* Is that the best you can do? Some kind of writer you are."

"Which, might I remind you, is how come we were able to make this appointment. There are very few times when being an author is useful, but it lends a certain legitimacy to any research project."

"It gives you an excuse to show off," Dan shot back. "Anyway, it worked, so I'm not complaining, but where is he, do you think, this Doctor Jenkinson chap? We're on time, aren't we?"

Alan checked his watch. "Yes. It was very good of him to see us at such short notice."

"Short notice? You sent an email five days ago. I'd almost given up hope."

"Yes, well unlike you, I tend to assume that other people have real lives to be getting on with. Not everyone can drop everything and hare off on a wild goose chase when the fancy takes them."

"Apparently," Dan said. "Anyway, there's an information desk over there. Why don't you go and have a word? It might get things moving."

"Good idea." Alan strode across to the front desk, leaving Dan to stare in wonder at the impressive entrance hall.

The woman behind the desk looked up with a friendly smile. "Good afternoon, sir. What can I do for you?"

"I'm Alan Hargreaves. I have an appointment with Doctor Jenkinson."

"Ah, yes." The woman checked her screen then lifted a telephone. "If you wait here, I'll let her know you've arrived."

"Thank you." Alan stood back while the call was made, and when Dan joined him, Alan leaned close, lowering his voice. "We've been guilty of sexism. Doctor Jenkinson is a woman."

"Oh. It was hard to tell from an email," Dan said. "Still, it's an easy mistake to make, and I didn't mean anything by it. I hardly think we're the forces of oppression."

"But we ought to have known better," Alan replied. "It's easy to dismiss the concerns of others when you're more privileged than they are."

Dan's gaze flicked upward. "You'll get no arguments from me. Hard to see it any other way when you're standing beneath a marble statue of Prince Albert."

"Oh, I think this might be her," Alan said, and they watched as a young woman emerged from a side room and marched toward them.

"Mr Hargreaves," she said with a smile. "I recognise you from your photo."

"Guilty," Alan said, pulling himself up to his full height. "And this is my research assistant, Dan Corrigan."

Dan's stare ought to have sliced Alan in two, but neither its target nor Doctor Jenkinson noticed.

"A pleasure to meet you," she said, and they shook hands. "I have to tell you, Mr Hargreaves, that my son, Jake, is a huge fan of your books. I think we have every single one of your Uncle Derek series. And of course, he has the same name as your young hero, so that's an added attraction." She paused for breath. "Sorry, I'm gushing, but he was so thrilled when I told him I was meeting you. I must get you to sign a book before you go, that's if you don't mind."

"No problem at all," Alan said. "I should be delighted."

"Great."

"I thought you said your son was called Jake," Dan chipped in, "but just now, you said he had the same name as...what was it...Uncle Eric? Which is it?"

Doctor Jenkinson turned to Dan. "How long have you been working for Alan?"

"Oh, not long at all," Dan replied. "In fact, it feels like only a minute since I started."

73

"He's only recently joined me," Alan explained. "Dan, you really must get up to speed. Uncle Derek, international explorer, is one of the main characters in my books, but as far as my fans are concerned, the real hero of the tales is his young nephew, Jake."

"Absolutely," Doctor Jenkinson said. "Derek usually ends up in trouble, but Jake is the one who saves the day." She rubbed her hands together. "So, what's in store for this thrilling instalment? Will Derek and Jake be setting off on a hunt across the globe for priceless ancient relics?"

"Actually, this is a new project," Alan said quickly. "I'd be grateful if you'd keep this under your hat, but I'm working on a project set around the First World War."

Doctor Jenkinson's eyes widened. "Oh, but in your email, you said you wanted to see the artefacts donated by the Kenning family."

"That's right."

"Well, I'm sorry to disappoint you, Mr Hargreaves, but as I said in my email, they're all from Ancient Rome."

Dan exchanged a look with Alan. "We were under the impression that there may be a few other items in the collection. Documents, personal items belonging to Gordon Kenning, that sort of thing."

Doctor Jenkinson favoured them with a patient smile. "As I'm sure you'll appreciate, my work here is very specialised. My field is ancient Rome, and if there were other items in the collection, they wouldn't have been passed to me." She let out a sigh. "I'm sorry, but it looks as though you've had a wasted journey, and I have a lot of work to get back to, so…"

Dan stepped closer to her, wearing his most charming smile. "I wonder, Doctor Jenkinson, do you think you might be able to put us in touch with the right person? We have come over here especially, and it would be a shame for Mr Hargreaves to go away empty-handed. We waited five days for this appointment, and he really is terribly busy with his writing schedule."

"I'm afraid not," Doctor Jenkinson started to say, but Dan carried on regardless.

"I'm sure that while we wait, Mr Hargreaves would autograph as many books as you'd like."

"Oh, yes," Alan said. "And please, call me Alan."

Doctor Jenkinson studied them in silence. "How long did you say you'd been working together?"

"A few weeks," Dan said, just as Alan blurted out, "A few days."

"Ah. I see." Doctor Jenkinson seemed to be struggling to suppress a grin.

"I don't know what you're thinking," Dan began, "but you're probably wide of the mark. The truth is, we're neighbours. We just happen to be working on a research project together."

"You're not his assistant?"

Dan shook his head.

"Then why the pretence?"

"I'm sorry to have led you up the garden path," Alan said. "I suppose I thought it would lend us a bit of credibility."

Doctor Jenkinson folded her arms across her chest. "Talk about a spectacular backfire."

Alan winced. "Yes. I really am sorry. It was foolish, and I shouldn't have allowed myself to get carried away."

"But, it is kind of funny," Doctor Jenkinson said, and when she looked at Alan, there was a twinkle in her eye. "In my bag downstairs, I have no less than twelve paperbacks that my son insisted I bring along today. I told him you wouldn't have time to sign more than one or two, but you know how children are."

Alan slipped his hand inside his pocket, and with a flourish, he produced a pen. "Would he like them all made out to Jake, or is there a special message he'd prefer?"

"Wait here." Doctor Jenkinson gestured toward a bench. "Take a seat while I see if I can call in a favour. *And*, I'm going to collect the books, so don't go anywhere. I won't be long." She walked away, striding purposefully across the hall, and once they'd dutifully taken up their positions on the bench, Alan ran his hand across his brow.

"I've never been so embarrassed in my life," he said. "What must she think of me?"

"Do you care?" Dan asked. "Mind you, she's an attractive woman, and obviously a fan. I saw the way she looked at you."

"She's probably married," Alan shot back.

"Not necessarily." Dan grinned. "Anyway, you've only yourself to blame if you've got off on the wrong foot. Honestly, who could ever believe that *I* was your assistant?"

"Plenty of people. Anyway, the last time I checked, you were the one in need of a job."

Dan's smile was tight, a muscle in his cheek twitching. "Touché." For a moment, an awkward silence hung in the air, then a movement across the hall caught Dan's eye, and he was relieved to see Doctor Jenkinson marching towards them, a bulging canvas tote bag dangling from her hand. And trailing in her wake was a man who fitted Dan's idea of a professional historian, right down to the white lab coat and the wire-framed spectacles.

"I think we might be in luck," Alan said, then he looked Dan in the eye. "I shouldn't have said that about your job. It was a low blow."

Dan shook his head. "No, I had it coming. I didn't mean to be..."

"Irritatingly superior?" Alan offered. "Self-satisfied? Conceited?"

"That'll do for starters," Dan said. "I'll tell you what, I'll buy you a pint and we'll call it quits, okay?"

"In the pub? You'll actually come out for a drink?"

"Definitely."

Alan rubbed his hands together. "It's a deal. Now, I'd better get signing books. I have a feeling that I'll have to finish the whole pile before we're allowed to take one step further, and if there are only a dozen books in that bag, I shall be very surprised."

"It'll be worth it," Dan said. "And if my theory about the good doctor is correct, you never know what might come of it."

"You're not going to say anything foolish, are you?" Alan asked, a hint of desperation in his voice. "For God's sake, let's keep this professional. I've been humiliated enough."

"Whatever you say," Dan said. "After all, I'm only a humble assistant." And before Alan had a chance to reply, Dan stood to greet Doctor Jenkinson and her colleague.

CHAPTER 10

Exeter

"It's just down here," Doctor Harrison said, leading Dan and Alan down a narrow stairwell and descending into the bowels of the Royal Albert Memorial Museum. "Almost there."

They emerged into a brightly lit corridor, but the historian did not slow his pace. "This is very kind of you," Alan said. "I hope we're not holding you up too much."

"I can give you half an hour," Doctor Harrison said over his shoulder. "To be honest, it's nice to take a break from my routine work." He stopped beside a plain white door, its surface unmarked. "This is one of our archives. You wouldn't normally have access, but Sally vouched for you, and that's good enough for me."

"I presume that Sally is Doctor Jenkinson's first name," Dan said, smiling at Alan.

"Yes," Doctor Harrison replied. "She's great, isn't she? She brightens this place up, I can tell you."

"Definitely," Dan said, but before he could go on, Alan said, "Will we need to wear white coats or anything?"

Doctor Harrison shook his head. "No. We don't even use gloves most of the time; they can make you clumsy. Anyway, I'll have to fetch the documents for you, and if anything's too fragile, I won't be handing it over I'm afraid. Conservation comes first, but so long as your hands are clean and dry, you'll be fine." He peered at them. "Your hands *are* clean, I take it?"

"Absolutely," Alan said, waggling his fingers in the air. "It's quite exciting, isn't it? The thrill of discovery, of delving into the distant past."

"It can be," Doctor Harrison replied, pulling open the door. "And then there are days when you hit one dead end after another. It's like panning for gold. You have to sift through a tonne of dirt to find the nuggets, but when you do, you feel like the work was worthwhile."

Dan's smile faded. "If we've only got half an hour, I suppose our chances of success are minimal."

"Oh, I don't know," Doctor Harrison said. "You already have your inquiry pinned down to one small collection, and from what Sally said, you're only interested in the Great War. In my field, that would be considered quite a precise starting point."

"Actually, we're only looking at the years immediately after the war," Alan explained. "1919 to 1920."

"Even better." Doctor Harrison extended his arm toward the doorway. "After you. It's a controlled environment, so I have to make sure the door is sealed once we're inside."

Dan and Alan filed into the room, gazing at the orderly rows and columns of white drawers lining both walls. "How many documents do you have in here?" Dan asked, his voice echoing eerily.

"One hundred and seventy-two thousand, five hundred and three," Doctor Harrison replied. "And that's just in this room. Now, if you'll follow me, I'll take you to the Kenning collection." He bustled past them, and they followed at his heels, Dan looking around, deep in thought.

The weight of history seemed to press in on him from the crowded rows of drawers. How many lives had left nothing behind but the sheets of crumpled paper carefully stacked in sealed compartments like this? And how many more souls had left even less of a mark on the world, their records discarded and left to crumble to dust, their lives fading from memory? Over the last few days, he and Alan had spent hours researching the aftermath of the First World War, and he'd lost count of the images of war graves that he'd seen. Across the fields of Belgium and France, the almost endless rows of headstones stood to attention as if waiting for an event that would never come. To this day, the cemeteries were tended and cared for, kept in immaculate condition, but the people who lay beneath the stones were gone, and the last veteran of those horrific battles had died some time ago. *We will remember them*, Dan thought, recalling the words spoken at every Armistice Day event. But while the flames of remembrance burned bright, the memories could only grow more abstract. *We mourn for a generation*, Dan decided, *but there's no one who can point to a headstone and say, "He was my friend."*

Gordon Kenning had lost his only brother, it was no wonder that he'd turned away from the military. But to become a recluse? To hide away in his country mansion collecting Roman artefacts that he knew to be fake? To hide his grief in a coded message?

There was something else here. From what Martin Kenning had said in the cemetery, it sounded as though Gordon had lost faith in all the institutions that had governed his life. Perhaps now, at last, they were going to find out why.

"Are you all right?" Alan asked quietly. "You've gone a bit pale."

Dan managed a noncommittal shrug. "I'm fine. It's just cold down here."

"Thirteen degrees Celsius," Doctor Harrison called out, "and a mere thirty-five percent relative humidity. If I'm going to be in here for long, I bring a coat." He stopped and turned to face them. "This is the right section. But before we dive in, if there's anything specific you're looking for, I can check the index and save a lot of time. Is it definitely 1919 and 1920 that you want?"

Dan nodded. "Yes. Anything belonging to Gordon Kenning would be great, but we're particularly looking for personal documents such as journals or correspondence."

"Over the last few days, we've learned a healthy mistrust of official sources," Alan added. "It's possible that Gordon's brother, Cyril, died of the Spanish flu, and we understand that the authorities suppressed the details at the time."

"Hence the name *Spanish* flu," Doctor Harrison said. "The authorities were keen to give the impression that the disease was particularly bad elsewhere, when in fact, the crowded military hospitals and trains ensured the illness spread rapidly through the troops. I suppose, these days, we'd call it *spin* or *fake news*, but there's nothing new about propaganda. Take it from me; I've seen screeds of the stuff. Mind you, it can be illuminating. It tells you what people were prepared to believe, which can provide valuable insights into the way they thought and acted."

"I'm sure you're right." Dan felt a twitch of impatience stirring in his gut. They were so close now, he couldn't wait another second. "All the same, we'll start with the personal documents, and if there's anything with a reference to Cyril Kenning, that would be great."

"Right. If you stay put for a second, I'll see what I can dig up from the index." Doctor Harrison hurried down the room to a desk at the far end, where he hunched over a computer, tapping rapidly at the keyboard.

"What do you think we'll find?" Alan asked Dan. "Will you be disappointed if it turns out that Martin has already told us everything?"

Dan hesitated. "I'd be very surprised if that turns out to be the case, but I don't think I'd be too disappointed. After all, in a funny sort of way, I've enjoyed the challenge. It's kept my mind busy for a while."

"Me too," Alan said. "I almost don't want it to be over."

"Wait and see. But it looks like we won't have to hang around much longer. He's coming back."

"And he looks pleased with himself." Alan chortled under his breath. "Do you think we'll have to show him that we've cleaned our fingernails?"

"At this point, nothing would surprise me."

"Right," Doctor Harrison said, striding towards them, waving a slip of paper. "We only need one drawer, so that's perfect." He scanned the wall then pulled a drawer from its slot, carrying it carefully across to a table in the centre of the room and laying it down. "Give me a second."

Dan and Alan hovered beside him, watching as he laid out a series of yellowing pages along the bench. "Can we pick them up?" Dan asked.

"Yes, but please be careful," Doctor Harrison said, "and you might not believe that I have to say this, but please, if you have to turn a page, don't lick your fingers. Sometimes, people do it without thinking."

"Noted," Dan said, bending over the bench. He scanned the text of the first document, but it seemed to be a typically mundane piece of family correspondence. The signature was on the second page, and Dan struggled to make it out. "Gordon's mother was called Hester, wasn't she?"

"Yes," Alan stated. "She lived until 1941, but she never remarried. We couldn't find out what happened to her husband. All we know about Timothy Kenning is that he died young, probably in 1905."

"You two have been doing your research," Doctor Harrison said while he laid out more pages along the bench. "Perhaps you've missed your vocations."

"Maybe," Dan replied without looking up. "We've done little else but search through websites for the last five days. When I close my eyes, I see names and dates, battles and hospitals, regiments and battalions."

"Tell me about it," Alan chipped in. "We've hunted high and low, but until now, we've been defeated. These documents are our last hope."

"Cyril will be in here somewhere," Dan said, moving on to the next document. "He and Gordon were close, so they must've exchanged letters."

Doctor Harrison grunted. "You're assuming the letters would've been kept. Do *you* keep all *your* correspondence?"

Dan straightened his back. "I don't have a lot, but I keep some of it: the ones that are important to me, letters from my parents."

"And what will happen to all those letters when you die?" Doctor Harrison asked. "Have you made arrangements for them to be preserved? And even supposing that your next of kin try to follow your wishes, one bundle of papers looks much like another. Will your descendants understand what they're looking at? And a hundred years from now, will your precious letters still exist?"

"Ah, I see what you're getting at." Dan chewed on his lower lip, unsure what to say.

"We idealise people in the past," Doctor Harrison went on, "but they were just like us, just as fallible. They couldn't have known how we'd judge them, nor did they know what we'd find important. So you might find what you're looking for, but there are no guarantees."

"Except, that I just have," Alan said, his voice unnaturally loud in the quiet room. "I've found *exactly* what we're looking for."

Dan and Doctor Harrison hurried to his side, and huddling together, they stared down at the single sheet of writing paper that Alan had pulled towards him.

To Captain G. Kenning, 24ᵗʰ March 1919, Dan read, but when his eyes went to the uneven handwriting on the next line, a chill ran down his spine.

I'm supposed to be writing to my dad, but he can't hardly read, and anyway, I wanted you to know that whatever they say about your brother, it most likely isn't true.

Dan's chest tightened as he read on:

We was both in the Calais hospital with the flu, but I was in a bad way. The doctors had a name for it, but all I know is, I wasn't myself, wasn't right in my mind. I had the fear of God in me. Not just scared, but something else. Something worse. I couldn't stop it, but Lieutenant Kenning, he took me under his wing. We'd both been in the 2nd Battalion, the Devonshires, you see, and there weren't many of us left. He tried to jolly me along, keep my spirits up. We'd have a fine time after the fighting was over, he'd say. I knew a gentleman such as him wouldn't want to be seen with someone like me when we got back to Blighty, but he'd have none of it. Things will be different, he'd say.

Dan reached the end of the page. "Can we turn it over?"

"Yes, yes," Alan replied, and with deft fingers, Doctor Harrison flipped the sheet of paper over.

I don't know how long I was in that place, but we were lucky, and we pulled through. It was more down to your brother than the doctors if you ask me, but at any rate, they reckoned we was fit for duty, and we got our orders around the same time. Lieutenant Kenning said it would be all right, but I went to pieces all over again. It shames me, but I ran away. He shouldn't have done it, but your brother came after me. He found me hiding in a barn, but I wouldn't go back with him. I'd stolen some clothes, thrown my uniform in a ditch, but he tried to talk some sense into me. He was a very patient man. Brave too. I told him to leave me there, but he wouldn't do it.

When the patrol found us, we'd only been away for a few hours, just talking. I wanted to own up, but your brother shouldered the blame, said it was all his fault. I tried to explain but nobody would listen. They said we were as bad as each other. Deserters.

In the morning, I'm to be shot, and that's that, but I fear for your poor brother because the guards won't tell me what's happening to him. The chaplain came to visit, and I begged him to tell me the truth, but he just said that things don't look good.

They're saying your brother was an officer and knew the score, so the chaplain thought they might be hard on the poor man, make an example of him. It isn't right. It just isn't right.

I don't know what else to say except I'm sorry. The chaplain said he'll take this letter for me, so I want you to know one thing. Your brother was the bravest man I ever knew, and if I get to meet him again in heaven, I shall gladly shake him by the hand.

Yours faithfully,

Peter Murphy, Private, 2ⁿᵈ Battalion, The Devonshires.

"Bloody hell," Dan muttered, and all three men straightened at the same time.

"This is awful," Alan said, his voice faint. "I can't get my head around it. That poor man. And what happened to Cyril? Would they really have shot him too?"

"Of course they did," Dan stated. "It's the only explanation that fits the facts. It's all there in the letter. Murphy said Cyril shouldered the blame. As an officer, he was clearly determined to take all the responsibility. And more than that, he wanted to stick by his friend, his brother in arms. They'd been through hell together, surviving a brutal battle and seeing most of their comrades killed."

"The defence of Bois des Buttes," Alan explained to Doctor Harrison. "The Second Battalion was all but wiped out. They were awarded the Croix de Guerre for gallantry."

"They fought to the bitter end even though they must've known they couldn't win," Dan said. "That tells you everything you need to know about Cyril Kenning. And even after the war, despite being struck down with the Spanish flu himself, he looked after Murphy, making sure he pulled through. When the odds were against him, Cyril dug his heels in. There's no way he would've walked away and let his friend down."

"You paint a very vivid picture," Doctor Harrison said. "As a historian, I prefer solid facts, but we often try to guess at what went on in the minds of those who are long gone. In this case, I'd say that your interpretation is as good as any. You certainly seem to have got under Cyril Kenning's skin. It's almost as if you knew him."

Dan hesitated. "We've been on his trail for a while, and he's been on my mind, always just ahead, out of reach. Now, we've finally caught up with him."

"Yes," Alan put in. "I feel as though I've spent a lot of time in Cyril's company. It's sad to think he might've ended his days in that dreadful way."

"There's no *might* about it," Dan said. "When they executed Murphy, Cyril's fate was sealed. That's why the Kennings don't want the story dragged up; they're ashamed to have a deserter in the family. It doesn't fit their heroic narrative." He paused, thinking. "Remember when Martin quizzed us about our intentions? I knew something was wrong when he started talking about social media. He really doesn't want the truth to get out."

"Why?" Alan asked. "What does it matter?"

"Pride," Dan said. "Loss of face. To men like David and Martin, being an officer isn't just a job, it defines them. I've seen the same kind of thing among the high-flyers in the city. When your life is built on your reputation, without it, you're nothing. Less than nothing."

Alan frowned. "But there's no reason for them to feel ashamed. This letter explains everything."

"When were Gordon's documents donated to the museum?" Dan asked Doctor Harrison.

"They were a bequest, so they would've been transferred shortly after his death."

"1972," Alan said. "That's quite some time ago. I wonder if David and Martin even know about the letter."

Dan shook his head. "I doubt it. You heard what they think of Gordon. Martin called him a crank, and they were keen to get rid of his collection of Roman artefacts, so I really don't think they'd bother to wade through his personal papers. Some things, it seems, they're very keen to forget."

"I still find all this hard to accept," Alan said. "Cyril survived so much. Could he really have been killed by his own side?"

Doctor Harrison sighed. "It happened. Not often, given the sheer number of soldiers, but around three hundred British soldiers were executed. Some for murder, but others for cowardice or desertion. And there were other crimes that carried the death penalty such as striking a superior officer or casting away their weapons. Murphy removed his uniform, and that may well have been enough to convict him. If Cyril insisted on taking responsibility, he would've been in deep trouble."

"But both men had been severely ill," Alan protested. "This Peter Murphy sounds like he had PTSD."

"That wasn't well understood, and anyway, it wouldn't have been taken into account in a case of desertion," Doctor Harrison said. "It was called shell shock or war neurosis, but no doctor would ever defend a deserter. I know it sounds inhuman to our ears, but that's how it was."

"Then it was barbaric and senseless," Dan growled. "This was after the armistice for God's sake. The fighting was over."

"Yes, but there were still huge numbers of troops across Europe," Doctor Harrison explained. "I suspect the authorities feared a slide into chaos. I'm not excusing their actions, but they were probably trying to maintain discipline in the only way they understood." He pulled off his glasses and rubbed his eyes. "That's if the letter is reliable, of course. It looks genuine, but personal accounts are hardly ever impartial."

Dan closed his eyes, trying very hard not to picture the last moments of Cyril Kenning's life, but the sensations came anyway: the sound of rifles being loaded, the slide of the bolt, the barked orders, the final report of gunfire as the pain seared through his mind, erasing his young life.

"Jesus," he whispered, opening his eyes. "If I'd known what we'd find, I don't think I'd ever have started on this, but now, I can see that it all fits. Cyril was shot for desertion, and it broke his brother's heart. They'd both trusted in the institutions of church and state, but neither helped Cyril. The army killed his brother, and a chaplain could do nothing except to send this letter. Gordon turned away from the church, throwing himself into his work, and when he became a recluse, the truth was lost. He must've decided that any attempt to clear his brother's name would've been futile. The war was over; no one wanted to know."

"The Great War touched almost every family in the country," Doctor Harrison said. "When so many had lost loved ones, any suggestion of cowardice would've been hard to live down."

Dan nodded. "And a generation later, the Kennings were so ashamed that they wrote poor Cyril out of their history."

"In his own way, though, Gordon tried to pay his respects to his brother," Alan said. "He might not have been able to talk about him openly, but he found a way to keep Cyril's memory alive, building a memorial that only he could understand."

"And maybe his business was a testament too," Dan added. "Cyril survived the flu pandemic, so in setting up pharmacies, Gordon was trying to bring healthcare to ordinary people. After all, there was no National Health Service back then."

Doctor Harrison cleared his throat. "I'm afraid that you're in danger of straying too far from the evidence, but if it's any consolation, I'd say that you've gleaned as much information as you can from this letter. And now, I really have to get back to work. If you want to go through anything else in the archive, you can always make an appointment. In the meantime, if you leave me your address, I can arrange for a copy of Murphy's letter to be sent to you."

"Yes, I'd like that," Dan said. "I'd like that very much."

"Could I have a copy too, please?" Alan asked. "Obviously, if there's a charge..."

"Don't worry about it," Doctor Harrison replied. "We'll call it *community outreach*, that covers most things. But, Sally said that you two were neighbours. It'll save on postage if I can send the copies to one of you."

"Oh, I don't know if that will work," Alan began. "You're heading back to London, aren't you?"

But Dan found himself smiling. "It's fine, Alan. Give Doctor Harrison your address, and when the letters arrive, just give me a shout, and I'll pop around to collect my copy."

"It might take me a few days to process it," Doctor Harrison warned. "There's a procedure. We have to use a special copier."

"That's all right," Dan said. "I'll be sticking around. I'm not sure how long for, but...we'll see."

"Okay. I'll just put the rest away, then I'll show you out." Leaving the letter to one side, Doctor Harrison began returning the documents to the drawer, keeping them in careful order. "So, what's your next line of inquiry? Are you sticking with the Kennings, or are you pursuing the Great War angle?"

Dan exchanged a look with Alan. Was there an eager spark of optimism in Alan's eyes, a glint of anticipation? Yes. And when he considered the prospect of solving another puzzle, something stirred in his soul in a way that it hadn't done for some time, and he found himself saying, "I think we'll start on something new."

"Excellent," Doctor Harrison said as he slid the drawer back into its home. "And what will be the focus of your next project?"

"I have no idea," Dan admitted. "Something will turn up, I expect, but first, we have an errand to run."

"Right, I'll take you back to the main entrance," Doctor Harrison said, and they followed him through the door, heading back to the impressive entrance hall.

When they'd said goodbye to Doctor Harrison, and Alan had left his address, Dan led the way outside, and they halted for a moment on the busy pavement. "What's this errand then?" Alan asked. "Have you got some shopping to do?"

"No," Dan replied. "I don't know about you, but I'm in the mood for a really good cup of coffee."

Alan's face fell. "Oh no, you don't want to head back to the Aquifer Café, do you? I really can't face another argument."

Dan shook his head. "No. In fact, I'm prepared to go pretty much anywhere else, but if I'm going to stick around for a while, I really must find a decent coffee shop. The hunt starts here, but I'll tell you what, why don't you get the ball rolling? You know the city, you can choose the first contender."

"Seriously?" Alan let out a chuckle. "In that case, I know just the place. I've been doing some research of my own. Come on. I'll show you." Alan set off at a good pace, and Dan strode alongside him, the two marching along the street in companionable silence.

Dan thought he recognised the narrow alley that Alan led him through, and when they emerged from the other end, he caught sight of a banner attached to the fence surrounding a schoolyard. "Ah, this is Sidwell. The area you told me about."

"Exactly," Alan said without slowing. "And look!" He pointed to a row of small shops, and there, looking as if it had been converted from an ordinary townhouse, was a café, its plate-glass windows adorned with neat white lettering:

The Eggplant Café
100% Vegan

"I don't know what the coffee is like," Alan said, "but it has some good reviews online. The cakes are supposed to be wonderful."

Dan halted. "This is...very thoughtful. Thank you."

"So what are we waiting for?" Alan gave Dan a gentle shove, urging him forwards. "Wait until you see inside."

And when they bustled in through the door, Dan couldn't help but stare. "I don't believe it."

"I thought you'd like it," Alan said, then he led the way across the room and leaned on the wrought-iron railing that separated the corner from the seating area. There, he pointed to the small water feature: a circle of stones surrounding a plastic tub of water. A few coins gleamed from beneath the surface, and the scene was decorated with artificial plants. "*This* is supposed to be the site of the well of Saint Sidwell. Whether anyone can be sure of that, I don't know, but at least it's in the right place, and the road we've just crossed is called Well Street, so it has a reasonable claim."

"Deborah stole the idea lock, stock and plastic barrel," Dan muttered. "What a nerve."

Alan nodded. "She's certainly dishonest, but there's not much we can do about it, and in the grand scheme of things, I'm not sure it really matters." He sent Dan a smile. "Now that we're here, we may as well try the coffee, and since you can eat anything from the menu, you can go mad. My treat."

For a moment, Dan's frown remained in place. But when Alan took a seat and began studying the menu, he found his sense of irritation slipping away. Deborah was a fraud, and the Kenning family were emotionally repressed and clinging for grim death to a way of life that made no sense in the twenty-first century. But if Alan could let it all go, then so could he. At any rate, it seemed worth a try.

Dan nodded, and as he went to join Alan at the table, he felt somehow lighter, as if a burden had slipped from his shoulders.

"They have cheesecake," Alan said, wiggling his eyebrows. "How on earth do they make that from plants?"

"I'm really not sure," Dan said, plucking another menu from its stand. "I say we find out, but only *after* I get my cup of coffee, and since you're buying, I'll have a large cup."

"Me too," Alan said. "Frankly, I think we've earned it."

CHAPTER 11

Town Cemetery, Bethune, Pas de Calais, France

His hands deep in his coat pockets, Dan walked along the row of head-stones. Alan walked at his side. There was no need to say anything. Once they'd found the details of Cyril Kenning's execution, it had been a simple matter to find the precise location of his last resting place, and now, Dan stopped in front of it, his head bowed.

They'd bought a small bunch of flowers, and though the mixed blooms seemed poor and inadequate, Dan laid them in front of the headstone.

For a minute, neither of them said a word, then finally, Alan broke the silence. "We ought to have brought poppies."

Dan shook his head. "We're here, that's what counts."

"Yes." Alan pulled a piece of paper from his pocket. "Do you mind if I read something?"

"No. I think that would be good."

Alan took a breath and then, in a loud, clear voice, he began:

"To My Brother.

Give me your hand, my brother, search my face;

Look in these eyes lest I should think of shame;

For we have made an end of all things base.

We are returning by the road we came.

Your lot is with the ghosts of soldiers dead,

And I am in the field where men must fight.

But in the gloom I see your laurell'd head

And through your victory I shall win the light."

Alan tucked the paper back into his pocket, and both men stared straight ahead, lost in thought.

Dan rubbed at the corners of his eyes. "He would've liked that. Gordon Kenning, I mean. I don't suppose he ever came here himself, but it feels right somehow."

"Yes. Unfinished business."

"It was good of you to come with me," Dan said. "And I'm glad you did. You read that very well."

"Thank you. Years of reading aloud to my class. I suppose you get a feel for it eventually. Not that this was the same." Alan hesitated. "What are you going to do with your copy of Private Murphy's letter? I thought I'd put mine in a frame and hang it up in the kitchen—somewhere where I'll notice it from time to time."

"My copy's gone," Dan said simply.

"What do you mean? You've lost it?"

"No. I don't hold on to things. I can't stand to drag all that clutter from place to place. So once I'd reread the letter a few times, I posted it; sent it to the one place where it might do some good."

Alan nodded thoughtfully. From his expression, it was clear that he didn't need any further explanation, and Dan was glad of it. They could talk later, but for the moment, the important thing was just to be there, to be present, and to stand, their heads bowed, in silence.

EPILOGUE

Knightsbrook House

In the quiet corner of the garden, Martin Kenning ran his hands over the slab of stone. It had cleaned up nicely, and the builder had done a good job of fixing it back in place. Deborah had complained, of course, when he'd removed it from her café, but he'd calmed her down and made her listen to reason. He'd told her to take down that nonsense about the saint too. She'd probably dream up some other fanciful tale to put in its place, but that couldn't be helped.

He thought of his own historical display back at the house. It was not without fault. He'd asked Arthur to remove Cyril's uniform from the display until he could figure out what to do with it. It raised too many questions, and the visitors to the estate wanted nothing more than a genteel day out in the English countryside; they weren't ready to face the realities of war. He'd probably donate the uniform to a military museum. There was one in the neighbouring county of Dorset, and they could make a proper job of telling Cyril's story. And told, it must be. There was no doubt about that.

In the meantime, Gordon's carved message was back in its rightful place, just where he'd wanted it. And below it, on the back of the new oak bench, a brass plaque gleamed in the sunshine, its message written out in plain English:

IN MEMORY OF CYRIL KENNING
A BELOVED BROTHER TAKEN TOO SOON
BY THE FOLLY OF A SENSELESS WAR.

*

Thank you for reading A Study in Stone. I really hope that you enjoyed it. At the back, I've included an afterword with some background notes, but in the meantime, you can keep reading with the first two chapters of the next Devonshire Mystery, Valley of Lies:

VALLEY OF LIES – CHAPTER 1

"Two pounds of liver!"

Standing at the bar in The Wild Boar, a full pint glass in each hand, Dan recoiled as the plastic packet of soft meat was thrust in front of his face. But despite his revulsion, he was unable to take his eyes from the grisly parcel of shrink-wrapped offal. Kevin, the landlord of Embervale's only pub, flexed his fingers, and the livid meat squirmed inside its transparent packet as if alive.

"What's the matter?" Kevin said. "Aren't you going to check your ticket? That's prime lambs' liver, that is. Tender. You might have the winning number. Three-nine-one."

"No, I didn't buy a ticket for the meat raffle." Dan was aware of the sidelong glances he was getting from the other customers, but he wasn't going to be intimidated. "I don't eat meat."

Kevin blinked slowly. Tall and heavily built, his rugged features and thick black beard giving him the look of a lumberjack rather than a landlord, the man seemed too large to be constrained behind the small bar. His eyes glittered darkly, and Dan fought the urge to step back. But then Kevin's features split in a wide smile, his strong teeth impossibly white against the raven black of his full beard. "Never mind. Perhaps we'll have a nut roast raffle one day, eh?"

There were murmurs of humourless laughter, enjoyment of an outsider's discomfort, and Dan turned to see a middle-aged man eyeing him with amused disdain. The man was average height, but he had the build of an athlete: an athlete gone to seed, perhaps, but an imposing figure, nevertheless. Dressed in a white T-shirt and faded denims, there was something predatory in the way the man leaned carelessly on the bar, his dark eyes locked on Dan in a calculated display of understated menace.

Dan bridled. In London, he'd go out of his way to avoid conflict, but here, in the sanctity of a small English pub in a quiet rural village, he shouldn't have to put up with this bullshit. Pulling himself up to his full height, he said, "Can I help you with something?"

The man held his gaze, unblinking, then he chuckled. When he spoke, his voice was hard, his flat vowels placing his origins firmly in the north of England. "Don't mind me. I wasn't laughing at you." He inclined his head toward the landlord. "Friendly bunch, aren't they? I've lived here for six years and they still treat me like the new boy." He straightened his back, offering his hand for a shake. "Name's Jay. Embervale's official Yorkshireman-in-exile."

Dan set down a glass and shook Jay's hand. "Nice to meet you. You must know Alan. He's from the north somewhere, I think."

Jay's smile tightened. "I know Alan Hargreaves, all right. But he's a scouser, isn't he? We don't call that north where I come from."

"And that would be Leeds."

"How did you know that?" Jay asked. "The lads back home reckon my accent went south when I did."

"You have it tattooed on your arm," Dan replied. "I suppose, LUFC could stand for something other than Leeds United, but the white rose gives it away."

Jay laughed, his hand going to his bicep to touch the small tattoo peeking out from his sleeve. "Fair play. I forget about the tats. It's been so long since I had them done."

Dan picked up his pint. "Well, I'd better get back with these drinks. Alan will be getting thirsty."

"That's right," Kevin said. "Don't waste good drinking time." He'd followed Dan's conversation with rapt interest, and now, he grinned in approval. "You and Alan have been in here a few times. Friend, is it? Visiting like?"

"Neighbour, actually. I'm at The Old Shop. It's my sister's place. I'm staying there for a while."

"Local then. As good as, anyway." The change in Kevin's attitude was instant, his features growing more animated, and he spoke quickly, his words blurring into each other in a rush. "Any time you feel like a drink, you come along. We're having a quiz tomorrow. Usually a good crowd for that. Starts around eight, but you'll want to get here before then, to get organised with your team and all that. We've a nice guest ale, should be ready for tomorrow night. *Gun Dog.* Brewed local. Just the job for these summer nights. Drinks lovely, it does."

Dan frowned, his mind racing to catch up with the rapid ebb and flow of Kevin's speech. Dan had assumed he'd have no difficulty with the Devon accent, imagining it was normal English only spoken a little slower. But he'd been in Embervale for a few weeks now, and it was clear that the locals had other ideas. They changed some words, invented new ones, and missed others out entirely. Dan found himself cast in the role of the slow-minded idiot who couldn't keep up, and he didn't like it at all. So instead of asking Kevin to repeat himself, he simply said, "Right. Thanks. Maybe. We'll see."

Kevin's smile seemed fixed, and he stared at Dan, expecting more.

"Hey, Kev!" someone called out. "Are you doing this raffle or what?"

Kevin looked away and, the spell broken, Dan made a beeline for his seat by the window. From behind him, Kevin called out, "And the winner of this beautiful liver is pink ticket, number three hundred and ninety-one!"

"Got it!" someone replied. Amid a barrage of murmured moans, an elderly man bustled through the crowd, holding a pink paper ticket aloft as though it were a communique from the Queen.

Dan set the pints on the table, retaking his seat on the red velour chair, and Alan looked up expectantly, his expression brightening. "At last. I was about to send out a search party." He took an experimental sip then sat back, watching as Dan tried his drink. "What did you have? Looks like IPA."

Dan took a long draught before replying. "Yes. It's not bad."

"IPA's all right, I suppose. It's the trendy drink at the moment, isn't it? Everybody keeps trying to invent some new variety of the stuff. Still, at least we've managed to wean you off the bottled beer."

"Nothing wrong with bottled craft beer. Each to his own." Dan took another long drink, then let out a murmur of content. "I'll give you one thing, though. This place is a damned sight cheaper than London. Whenever I get a round in, I keep thinking they've got the price wrong."

"You should try the Jail Ale, like me. It's that bit stronger, so you get even more bang for your buck." Alan cast a sideways look at the bar. "I see you've been making friends with the locals. What did Jay have to say for himself?"

"Not much. The man has a chip on both shoulders. He seemed to know you, but not, I'd guess, in a good way. Which is odd, because you seem to be on good terms with everyone."

Alan shrugged. "Jay's all right, I suppose. But I've never been quite sure what he does for a living. People say he's an ex-copper, but he doesn't seem to have a regular job. He's in here most nights, flashing the cash, buying drinks for people. I reckon he keeps this place afloat single-handed. But there's always an ulterior motive with him, always something he wants in return. Do you know what I mean?"

"Oh yes. I know the type." Dan looked around the room. The raffle was still in full swing, and a young woman was proudly showing her friends her prize: an oddly shaped hunk of shrink-wrapped meat big enough to feed a family of six. "This raffle, do they really do it every week?"

"Yes. It's surprisingly popular. I don't usually take part, though. I don't have much use for big lumps of meat when I'm on my own."

"Thank goodness for small mercies. If I had to spend the evening with a chunk of raw meat sitting on the table, I might be tempted to make my excuses and leave. Especially on a warm night like this. It can't be hygienic."

Alan shrugged. "It's all vacuum-packed, and it's never done the locals any harm. At any rate, no one's died yet."

A yell from across the room made them both sit up with a start. A small knot of customers surrounded some kind of scuffle, and Kevin was already striding out from behind the bar, his broad shoulders back. "Enough of that," he boomed. "I'll have none of that behaviour in here."

A man in his early twenties stepped back from the crowd, his face pale, his hair tousled, and his rat-like features twisted into an evil sneer. "He started it, Kev. Mouthing off, as per bloody usual. Ask anyone." He pointed, and Dan recognised the accused as the elderly man who'd won the liver.

"I've done nothing," the old man protested. "You bloody people are all the same. Nothing but a bunch of lazy bastards. Nothing better to do than gossip behind a man's back. Following me around, poking your noses in, making your snide little threats. Well, I won't stand for it, do you hear me? I won't bloody stand for it!"

Kevin folded his arms, then he fixed the old man with a stern look. "I reckon you've had enough for one night, Morty. Come back another day when you've cooled down. But you'll mind your manners or you'll not be served, understand?"

"It's Mr Gamble to you," the old man snapped. "And I don't have to stand here listening to all this rubbish. I won't waste another minute of my time on you bloody people. I'm going, all right, and to hell with the lot of you." Turning on his heel, he marched away, and pausing only to nod to a grey-haired woman sitting alone at a table beside the door, he swept outside.

Kevin cast a warning glance at the group of young men, then he strode back to his position behind the bar, his expression unreadable. The background buzz of conversation resumed, but now, there was an undercurrent of snickering derision, and the young man's friends were slapping him on the back, laughing. They were pleased with themselves and already retelling the story, no doubt building the petty argument into a confrontation on a much grander scale.

But Dan found his attention going back to the grey-haired woman beside the door. Despite Morty's obvious rage, he'd taken the time to nod to her; he'd made a point of it. And yet the lady hadn't met his eye. Instead, she'd sat erect, almost regal, her sombre gaze focused on no one in particular. It must've taken some effort to assume such an air of cool indifference when the peace of the quiet pub had been disturbed right in front of her. But nevertheless, she'd managed it.

And there was something else: a tiny gesture that had almost gone unnoticed. But it had piqued Dan's interest, and he watched the woman for a minute before turning to Alan. "Do you know that lady? The one by the door."

Alan nodded. "That's Marge. At least, that's what most people call her, though it had better be *Mrs Treave* or *Marjorie* if you speak to her. Why?"

"I'm not sure. Does she know the man who stormed out just now? Are they friends?"

"I don't know. They're of the same vintage, you might say, and they're both local. She lives in The Old Buttery. It's a lovely old cottage, or it could be with a bit of work to modernise the plumbing and such. She must be acquainted with Mortimer, but that's probably as far as it goes. Marge keeps herself to herself, as you can probably see." He took a drink. "Why do you ask?"

Dan wrinkled his nose. "Probably nothing."

"Oh, no it isn't." Alan leaned forward, lowering his voice. "What is it? What did you see this time?"

"It's not a party trick," Dan said. "I can't help it if I'm more observant than most people. It's just the way my mind works."

"I disagree. You're an inveterate people-watcher. You work at it. I've seen you do it." Alan clicked his fingers. "That woman in John Lewis. You were dead right about her. I didn't believe you for a second. She looked like such a nice, middle-class lady, but you had her number. Half an hour later, there she was, being led out in handcuffs. Caught shoplifting, just like you predicted."

Dan chuckled under his breath. "Oh please. One look at her shoulder bag was enough for me. It's one thing to sport a Mulberry calf's leather bag on a trip to the West End, but for an afternoon trudging around Exeter? And anyway, it had been repaired, very badly. Then there were the stains on her skirt. Anyone could see the woman had fallen on hard times, but she still craved luxury. Do you see?"

"So she visited an upmarket shop, knowing she couldn't afford to buy," Alan said. "The poor woman."

"A thief. And I wouldn't call John Lewis upmarket. I suppose, for Exeter, it's high-end, but..."

"Here we go," Alan said. "Nothing around here quite matches up to London. We're all just peasants with no clue about anything."

"Oh, come on. I've never said anything like that."

"You've implied it often enough."

"Well, if I've offended you, I'm sorry," Dan said. "But that's never been my intention."

The two men eyed each other warily until Alan broke the silence. "I fancy some crisps." He stood. "Do you want anything? I don't know which ones are vegan, I'm afraid. Presumably not the cheese and onion."

"That's right, but funnily enough, the meat flavoured ones are usually fine. No meat in them at all." Dan smiled. "If they have them, I like the chilli flavour. That would be great, thanks."

"No problem." Alan headed to the bar, and Dan sat quietly, sipping his pint. But his gaze wandered back to Marjorie Treave. She was watching the group of young men, following their conversation. And in such a small way that almost no one would notice, she was smiling to herself.

Alan was right, Dan thought. *I do have a tendency to watch people, looking for clues.* It wasn't a habit he'd consciously acquired—it was more of a natural ability—but in his old job in the city, his flair for perceptive observation had stood him in good stead.

He'd been involved in scores of high-stakes negotiations, and unlike the showdowns between heroic individuals depicted by Hollywood, clashes in the boardroom were always crowded and messy affairs: competing groups vying for some advantage, jockeying for position, constantly probing the boundaries of the debate to see what they could get away with. In these situations, a fleeting glance, a twitch at the corner of a lip, or a tightening of the muscles around the eye could speak volumes. Dan had grown adept at noticing such things.

Like now, for instance, as he watched the carefree way Alan sauntered back from the bar, he knew that the storm clouds of disagreement had passed. Alan was an open book: slow to anger and quick to forgive and forget. Sure enough, Alan grinned as he tossed a packet of crisps onto the table. "Thai chilli. I asked Kev to check the ingredients very thoroughly, just to see his face. Priceless."

"Thanks. How much do I owe you?"

Alan waved his words away as he sat down. "Don't worry about it. You can get the snacks next time."

"Deal."

They sat in companionable silence for a while, crunching on crisps and sipping their drinks, until Alan said, "Okay, it's driving me mad and I have to know. What did Marge do that was worth noticing? Because I didn't see a thing, and I have to admit, if it was anything outlandish, I'd be surprised. Very surprised indeed."

"On the face of it, it wasn't anything shocking. But when the old man nodded to her, she didn't make eye contact with him. She shook her head ever so slightly. Just enough to mean *no*."

"No? Well, that makes sense. She probably thought Morty was making a fool of himself, and I expect she didn't approve. Marge is a quiet sort of person. Polite but very reserved."

"No, it wasn't disapproval," Dan said. "It was more definite than that. A signal, or an instruction, perhaps even an order."

"Good luck to her if she's trying to take Morty in hand. He doesn't take a blind bit of notice of anyone, and he doesn't care who he rubs up the wrong way. He shouted at me in the street once, apparently under the impression I'd pinched something from his front garden."

"And had you?"

"No. Of course, I hadn't. I stopped to admire his roses for a second, that was all. The next thing I knew, the old fool was yelling at me through the window." He laughed under his breath. "I just gave him a smile and a friendly wave. There was no way I was going to give him the satisfaction of spoiling my day."

"Always forgive your enemies; nothing annoys them so much," Dan said. "Oscar Wilde."

"Yes, I've always liked that one. But seriously, do you really think mousy little Marge can boss a man like Morty around? I can't see it myself."

"But I *did* see it. I'm sure of it. The question is, what was she saying no to?"

Alan tilted his head to one side. "Unless... No. You don't think she meant *not tonight*, do you? As if she was turning him down, fending off his passionate advances."

"These things happen. It's a small village. People get lonely."

"Yes, but those two? I'm not being ageist, but I can't see them as the Romeo and Juliet of Embervale." Alan glanced over at Marjorie. "She's a nice lady. A gentle soul really. You often see her out walking across the fields. She goes for miles. I think she picks wildflowers because she always seems to have a trug on her arm. That's a kind of wide basket."

"I know what a trug is," Dan said. "My mother had one. But you're not helping your argument. It sounds to me as though she's a romantic character, so why shouldn't she fall in love?"

"No reason at all. She lives alone, and so does Morty, but honestly, you saw what he's like. Obnoxious. Maybe he has a grudging respect for Marge, but I'm willing to bet that's all there is to it."

"Don't look now," Dan said. "She's leaving." He watched Marjorie Treave straighten her tweed skirt as she stood, then she picked up her empty sherry glass and headed for the bar.

"Wrong again," Alan said in a stage whisper. "She's going for a refill. She has a taste for dry sherry."

But Dan didn't reply. He was taking in the stately way she crossed the room, her posture proudly upright. Instead of making a detour around the gaggle of young men gathered beside the pub's only fruit machine, she marched into their midst. If she was intimidated by their open-mouthed stares, it didn't show in her haughty expression. But before any of the young men could speak, she fixed her eyes on the individual who'd badgered Morty.

"Steven Holder, you ought to be ashamed of yourself, boy," Marge snapped, her voice edged with steel. "I knew your mother, God rest her soul, knew her like she was my own daughter. I can tell you, she'd be sore disappointed in you, boy. Carrying on like that, tormenting poor old Mr Gamble. It's a disgrace. Pure and simple."

Every head in the room turned to watch Marjorie's speech, but no one said a word.

One of Steven's friends started to laugh, and Dan held his breath, his whole body tensing. The mood of the young men was already shifting, an ugly hatred in their eyes. Dan was no barroom brawler, but he could handle himself well enough, and there was no way he'd stand back and let an elderly woman go unprotected. Thankfully, he wouldn't be alone in stepping forward: Alan was already pushing back his chair, ready to move.

"Shut up!" Steven barked. But his anger was not directed at Marjorie. He was glaring at his snickering friend, his hands forming into fists. "Shut your gob, you stupid bastard!"

All the young men took half a step back from each other, eyes flicking around the group as they weighed the odds, chose sides.

Dan started to stand, but Alan laid a restraining hand on his arm. "It's all right," Alan muttered. And when a loud voice boomed across the bar, Dan understood.

"Now, now, children," Kevin called out, shouldering his way into the throng. "Behave yourselves, boys and girls. Don't make me knock some sense into your thick heads." He bared his teeth in the parody of a smile, the fierce glint in his eyes saying he'd like nothing better than to be provoked.

Steven scowled, shaking his head, but his friends had seen enough. "Come on, Steve," one of them said. "Let's get out of here. We can go around mine. I've got plenty of lagers in."

Steven fixed Kevin with a look, then he nodded to his friend. "Yeah, all right. I'm sick of this place, anyway. The beer tastes like rat piss." He threw a scowl around the room, then he made for the door, his friends following behind.

Kevin held out his hand to Marjorie, indicating her glass. "Can I take that for you, m'dear? Refill? On the house."

Marjorie thought for a moment. "No, I don't think so. I've had enough sherry. But since you're paying, I'll have a G and T. And just for taking such a casual tone with me, you'd better make it a double."

Kevin's bellowed laughter broke the tension, and as others joined in, more than one person gave a cheer. Kevin returned to his position, and Marjorie hoisted herself onto a bar stool, perching on its edge as she waited for her drink.

In seconds, the scene had returned to normal, and Dan shared a look with Alan. "Is it always like this on a Friday night?"

"Certainly not," Alan replied. "It's usually much more exciting and dramatic."

"Really?"

"No. Don't be silly. It was a joke."

"Thank God for that," Dan said. "I don't want to go through that again in a hurry. I thought we were about to have a murder on our hands."

"Yes. Marge is a tough old girl, but I wouldn't have given much for her chances against that lot. Still, it would never have come to that. We'd have stepped in, and I dare say a few more would've helped."

Dan took a gulp of his drink. Then another. He was thinking about the way Steven Holder had hung his head when Marge had scolded him, turning on his own friend for laughing at her. Dan looked at Marjorie with fresh eyes. Here was a formidable lady: not some frail senior citizen, but a woman with authority. A woman with power. And she was very careful and very calculating in the way she chose to wield her influence.

Fascinating, he thought. *There's something going on here. Something below the surface, something I can't quite see.*

And when he took his eyes from Marjorie, he saw that she was the focus of someone else's attention. Jay was staring at her from his place along the bar. There was a cold darkness in his glare: a gleam of...what? Resentment? Suppressed anger?

The man was holding back a deeply felt emotion, but what lay at its heart, Dan couldn't decide. He only knew that whatever it was, it sent a shiver to run down his spine.

VALLEY OF LIES – CHAPTER 2

The night was still warm as Dan walked back from the pub with Alan. There'd been no further incidents or upsets, and together, they'd spent a pleasant few hours, talking about nothing in particular and sharing a joke or two.

They left Fore Street, turning into the narrow lane that led down to their houses, and Dan stopped, looking up at the night sky and breathing deep. "I can't get used to the stars. So many."

"It's the lack of light pollution." Alan joined him in admiring the heavens. "You should see it in winter. On a clear frosty night, the milky way is fantastic."

Dan didn't reply. *I'll be long-gone before winter*, he thought. *Back to London and night skies obliterated by a dull orange glow*. But he didn't want to linger on thoughts of his real home, and anyway, it would be churlish to spoil the moment. So he stood, gazing upward, and listened patiently while Alan pointed out a few constellations, old memories stirring in the back of his mind.

"I used to do this when I was little," Dan said. "My dad used to show me the planets and constellations. Sometimes, we'd go out in the garden and he'd shine a torch up into the sky, tracing out the shapes, over and over again until I could see them."

"Ah, that's a nice memory. Is he...?"

Dan looked down. "Yes, he's still alive, but Mum and Dad are separated."

"I'm sorry to hear that. I didn't mean to pry."

"It's all right. They split up six years ago. Mum went to live in Brighton and Dad moved to the Lake District. I think they were trying to get as far away from each other as possible without actually leaving the country. They parted amicably enough, but it makes it hard to see them as often as I'd like. I must visit them both soon. Especially Dad; it's been ages."

"It's a long and tortuous drive to the Lake District from this part of the world," Alan replied. "Beautiful when you get there, though. He'll be pleased to see you."

"Yes. But you know how it is. He'll want to know what I'm doing with my life. And since I left my job..."

"It's more like your job left you," Alan said. "If you ask me, you're well out of it."

"Maybe." Dan hesitated. "How about you? Are your parents still alive?"

"Mum and Dad are down in Cornwall. A cottage by the sea."

"Sounds idyllic," Dan said, and a slight pang of envy drew tight in his stomach. Although they were about the same age, Alan's life was so much more ordered than his. Alan lived in a cosy little house, everything neat and in its proper place. Although he never boasted, Alan was doing well. Dan had looked online, and Alan's adventure stories for children were popular, selling all around the world. They were a big hit with parents and teachers too. There was talk of prizes and awards. And now this: the perfect set of proud parents living in the neighbouring county in a cottage by the sea. *Still, there's no sense in being jealous*, Dan told himself. *Good luck to him.*

Breaking in on his thoughts, Alan said, "What did you think to that last pint?"

"I think," Dan said, laying his hand on his stomach, "I think I probably shouldn't have had it."

Alan chuckled. "But the Jail Ale, what did you think of it?"

"It was good. Better than I expected. I see what you mean about it being stronger, but it was nice."

"Say what you like about Kev, but he keeps a good cellar."

"In that case, I'll say that for a big man, Kevin has very small feet. And very fancy shoes."

"You and your shoes. What are they, running shoes or something? I must say, I can't see Kev pounding the streets in Lycra."

"Nobody runs in Lycra anymore. Anyway, that's not what I meant." Dan scratched his chin. "I've lost my thread. Where was I?"

"Kevin's fashion sense, or lack of it."

Dan clicked his fingers. "Ah! I've just remembered. I was supposed to tell you something. When I got the last round in, Kevin said you'd left your hiking stick behind. The last time we were in, after that walk on Wednesday, you left it on the floor."

"Damn. I'm always leaving it somewhere or other. I suppose it's too late to go back for it now."

"I wouldn't bother. He's put it behind the bar for you." Dan offered an apologetic smile. "I meant to tell you, but then you got onto that joke about the camels, and for some reason, it slipped my mind."

"That's my standby joke," Alan said. "I keep it in reserve for emergencies."

"I'm not sure how to take that. I'm flattered you've shared one of your limited supply of jokes with me, but on the other hand, I'm slightly offended that an evening in my company represents some form of emergency."

"Well, if I'm honest, you were getting a bit maudlin, banging on about some girl or other."

"*Some girl?*" Dan puffed out his chest. "Frankie Herringway has been described as many things, but no one, not since she cast aside her knee-high hockey socks in favour of a Beverly Hills haute couture business suit, has anyone referred to her as *a girl*."

"And *that* is why I broke out the camel joke. No sense in moping over a woman you broke up with months ago. Move on; I'll bet she has."

"Easy for you to say."

"Meaning what?" Alan asked. "I haven't always been single, you know. I do have some idea about women."

"It's hardly the same. The height of sophistication in this village is wearing wellies that match your thorn-proof waxed jacket."

"And what's wrong with that? Personally, I prefer to spend my time with someone who has their feet on the ground: someone who understands what's really important in life. It's all very well knowing one pair of shoes from another, but what good are your Johnny Choos when your car breaks down in the middle of Dartmoor and it's a twenty-mile hike before even the fanciest new phone can get a signal?"

The two men locked eyes, but it wasn't long before a burst of laughter escaped from Dan's lips. "You're right. It's Jimmy Choo, by the way, not Johnny, but your point still stands. Not everyone in London is posh, far from it, but in the company I kept... Let's just say that when I lost my job, the silence was deafening."

"You'll get back on your feet soon enough, you'll see. A few more nights in the pub, and you'll be rehabilitated entirely." Alan laughed under his breath. "We had a good night, didn't we? The threat of a punch-up notwithstanding."

"Yes." Dan smiled, looking back along the street toward the pub, and a movement caught his eye: a solitary figure marching along the side of the road, the person casting a long shadow as they marched away from the lonely beam of the only working streetlight. "Speaking of which, that looks like Marjorie."

"Yes. On her way home." Alan raised a hand in greeting, but Marjorie Treave was intent on her purpose, looking neither to the left or the right, and she passed them by, oblivious to their presence.

They watched her as she turned from the main street, making her way into a quiet lane that led away from Embervale. The lane's pitted tarmac was just wide enough to admit a car, and Marjorie quickly disappeared into the deep shadows that lingered beneath the tall hedgerows.

"Should we let her go down there alone?" Dan asked. "She doesn't even have a torch."

"She's all right. She lives right on the edge of the village. Her place stands on its own. A little way down that lane, there's a public footpath to one side. You'd miss it unless you knew it was there. It leads across a couple of fields, then it goes past Marjorie's cottage. It's not far, and she's made that journey many times over the years. She could probably walk it with her eyes closed."

"Even so, it doesn't seem right. Anything could happen."

Alan held out his hands. "Like what? How many cars have passed while we've been standing here?"

"None. But anyone could be wandering about down there. Those lads from the pub; they'd know that she'd come this way."

"Steve isn't that bad," Alan said. "I know he looks a bit rough around the edges, but it's all talk: a show of bravado. I don't think he'd hurt anybody. He'll be round at a mate's house drinking warm lager and watching football."

Dan grunted under his breath. "I suppose you're right. Anyway, Marjorie wouldn't thank me if I offered to walk her home."

"Definitely not. And you wouldn't want to go bumbling about near her house at this time of night. Her geese would probably attack you."

"She has geese?" Dan asked. "Strange."

"Not really. Quite a few people keep them. The eggs are wonderful. She has chickens too, and a goat. She grows all her own veg. They say she's pretty much self-sufficient. She even keeps bees."

"A menagerie. She looks after all that on her own?"

Alan nodded. "Sure. Well, it's about time I turned—"

Alan's words were cut short by a guttural yell: a man's voice, strained to breaking point, a furious full-throated roar echoing along the empty street.

"Marge!" Alan said, his face pale. "That came from the field she goes through."

"I'm not sure," Dan said, turning, listening hard. Waiting. "The echoes...it's hard to tell."

Another shout: "Get out of here! Go!" And this time, he knew Alan was right. The yells were definitely coming from the direction where Marjorie had headed.

"Come on." Dan set off, running into the lane's dark mouth, Alan hard on his heels.

Another burst of outraged hollering rolled through the still night air, the words lost in a babble of incoherent rage. Dan ran faster, spurred on as the cries of anger gave way to howls of anguish. He couldn't see where he was going, and he almost turned his ankle as his feet found a pothole. But he ran on, his breath thick and fast in his throat, his heart hammering. He'd missed his regular runs for the last few days, and now he cursed his own laziness. His head spun, his legs unsteady as he raced over the uneven surface. The beer he'd so enjoyed, now churned in his stomach, his gut cramping, but he pushed the sensation aside and ran on. A thin branch whipped across his face, narrowly missing his eye, but he didn't slow his pace.

A blue-white light glimmered on the tarmac: Alan using his phone as a flashlight. *Good idea.* But Dan didn't stop to take out his own phone. "Where's the footpath?"

"Wait," Alan called out from behind him. "I'll have to show you."

"There's no time!" But Dan had no choice; he'd never find the path on his own. He staggered to a halt, breathing hard. "Quickly. It's gone quiet." He turned around, but the only sound was Alan's footsteps as he hurried to catch up.

"Wait a minute." Alan gasped for air. "Whoever it is, they could be anywhere. Once you stray from the path, there's nothing but fields for miles."

"We have to start somewhere. Show me the path." Dan fumbled for his phone and switched on the flashlight, playing its white beam along the hedgerow.

Alan strode past him. "Here! It's here." He clambered up the bank as if climbing into the hedgerow, but when Dan joined him, he saw a narrow wooden gate set back from the lane, and an algae-streaked sign pointing to the open space beyond.

Alan barged through the gate, Dan right behind him. "Which way?" Dan shone his phone's flashlight across the expanse of tall bracken that stretched out on either side, but its pale beam was swallowed up by the darkness.

"It's right in front of us." Alan urged him onward, indicating a faint path with his flashlight: a thin cleft in the towering bracken. Dan crept forward, unnerved by the oppressive darkness beyond his flashlight's meagre beam. The bracken's soft fingers dragged against his legs as he passed, and flying insects, attracted by the light, fluttered in front of him, danced erratically from side to side, then flitted away. A sudden breeze stirred the bracken, the fronds shushing gently against their neighbours, and brigades of crickets chirred in a demented whispering symphony. Something whined in Dan's his ear, and startled, he flapped it away then immediately felt foolish.

"Can you see anything?" Alan asked.

Dan stopped. "No. What's happened to Marjorie? She's nowhere in sight."

"It's not far to her house. She might've made it home before all that shouting started."

"I hope so." Dan started forward, but a soft sound rose over the crackling rhythm of their footsteps, and he stopped in his tracks. From somewhere in the expanse of swaying bracken, a low cry was carried on the breeze, and the murmured moan was heavy with despair.

"This way!" Dan struck out across the bracken, taking great strides. The vegetation was taller here, as high as his chest, but he pushed the stems aside and moved on.

"We're headed toward the spoil heaps," Alan said. "Whoever it is, they must be up there."

"What kind of spoil heaps? Are they dangerous?"

"There were mines out here. Silver and lead. They say the spoil heaps are safe, but nothing grows on them. It's not a place I'd want to hang around, especially after dark. Maybe I should call an ambulance. If someone's fallen…"

Dan took a breath. "Give it a minute. It might be nothing: kids mucking about, a drunk."

Another moan, quieter this time, and though the breeze made it hard to pinpoint the source of the sound, Dan broke into a jog, Alan following close behind.

Soon, the bracken gave way to gravel, the stones crunching underfoot. In front of them, rising sharply from the landscape, ridged banks of stony grey earth climbed into the night, the rugged slopes bleak and naked. Against the backdrop of lush vegetation, the spoil heaps' sterile surface seemed otherworldly, as if a chunk of the lunar landscape had been smuggled back to Earth in the dead of night.

"Hello?" Alan called out at the top of his voice. "Is anyone up there? We're here to help."

There was no reply.

"They must've heard that," Dan said. "Either they're unconscious, or they don't want to be found."

"So what do we do? Do we climb up?" Alan shone his light along the spoil heaps. "These things are huge. I don't know where to start."

"Look for footprints. A track. Anything. You go that way, and I'll head in the opposite direction. If you see anything, shout."

"Will do," Alan said, and moving slowly, they separated to skirt the lower edge of the heaps, the gravel rasping beneath their shoes with every step.

Dan had rarely felt so alone, so exposed. But at the same time, he was exhilarated, a savage sense of excitement thrilling through him. This was real. It meant something. He'd faced physical challenges before, but nothing could compare to this. For the first time in his life, the fate of another human being hung in the balance. If he failed now, a man may die.

"Hey!" It was Alan, his voice sharp. "Over here! Quick!"

Dan sprang into action, haring along the slope's edge, arms pumping. Ahead, Alan's phone bobbed in the darkness, loose stones skittering down the slope as he clambered up the unforgiving terrain. Dan dashed toward him, covering the distance in seconds. And there, on the slope, a dark shape lay immobile. A figure. A man.

Alan reached him first and crouched at his side. "Mr Gamble," Alan said, then again, raising his voice: "Mr Gamble! Mortimer, can you hear me? Are you all right?"

Dan slowed as he reached them, squatting next to the stricken figure and shining his light along the man's body. He wasn't sure what he was looking for, but he saw no obvious signs of injury. Mortimer Gamble's face was pale, streaked with dust, but he seemed placid, his eyes closed, and Dan felt a flood of relief; it could've been so much worse.

"He's alive," Alan said. "I'm calling an ambulance. Don't try to move him. His head..." He stepped away, lifting his phone to make the call.

There's nothing wrong with his head, Dan told himself. *He must be stunned, that's all.* But when he stood and walked carefully around the unconscious figure, Dan's breath caught in his chest.

Mortimer Gamble had suffered a terrible wound to the side of his head, and a thin trail of dark blood still trickled from a deep gash above his ear. The bleeding had almost stopped, but he'd lost enough blood to form a broad stain on the ground, and Dan was forced to accept the facts that his mind had tried to reject. Mortimer's body was limp, his features robbed of their natural expression, his face ashen. Dan could hear Mortimer's shallow, halting breath, but the old man seemed unbearably frail, as though he was already slipping into death.

"We're getting someone to help you," Dan said, hoping Mortimer would hear him. When he shone his light on the man's face, Mortimer's eyelids twitched. "Don't try to move," Dan went on. "Stay very still. You've hurt your head, but help is on its way. It's very important that you don't move."

A wheezing whisper escaped from Mortimer's lips, and Dan leaned close. "Mr Gamble, don't try to talk. Save your strength."

But Mortimer's eyes fluttered open, just a slit, squinting into the light, and Dan moved his flashlight away.

"Stop them," Mortimer whispered.

"Stay calm," Dan began, but it seemed as though Mortimer couldn't hear him.

"Don't let them get away with it," Mortimer said, his face pinched in pain. "I'm begging you. Stop them. Whatever it takes. Stop them."

"All right," Dan said. "Whatever it is, don't worry about it. Just lie still."

And with a long, rattling sigh, Mortimer Gamble closed his eyes.

*

That's the end of the preview, but you can find Valley of Lies online at:

books2read.com/valleyoflies

AFTERWORD – A STUDY IN STONE

This story is my first mystery, and although there were certainly challenges along the way, I enjoyed writing it immensely. I had some fun with the characters of Corrigan and Hargreaves, and at this point, I feel like they've limbered up and now they're raring to go. This pair have a certain chemistry, and I'm looking forward to throwing some more problems at them. I hope you're looking forward to more mysteries too.

In the meantime, here are a few notes that I hope will answer any questions you may have. I've also provided a list of reference links on my blog, so if there's a particular aspect that interests you, you can follow it up:

mikeycampling.com/a-study-in-stone-references/

Is Embervale a real place?

This story is set in the Dartmoor area where I've lived for over twenty years, but the village is entirely fictional. When I've used real places such as Exeter and Bovey Tracey, I've fictionalised them to some extent. I used the real name for the church in Bovey Tracey, but the names on the gravestones are fictional. The Aquifer Café is entirely fictional, but the Eggplant Café is inspired by a real-life vegan café in Exeter, and yes, they do have a well in one corner. In Exeter, the museum is real, but I've never been lucky enough to see behind the scenes, so I had to imagine that setting.

Was there really a Saint Sidwell?

The legend of Saint Sitwell hasn't been altered for this book, but like any legend, there are several versions of the tale. Sidwell is the patron saint of Exeter, and there is still an area of the city named after her.

How about Knightsbrook House?

This is a fictional stately home, but it has been inspired by several National Trust properties here in Devon. Ugbrooke House can only be visited via a guided tour, and they have a small military museum. Castle Drogo was built on the proceeds of commerce, but a chain of grocery stores was the source of wealth rather than pharmacies. Knightshayes is a grand house that lent part of its name to the story.

Are the military details real?

This is a tricky area to get right, but I wanted to use real regiments. The Second Battalion of the Devonshire Regiment were awarded the Croix de Guerre for their outstanding bravery, and the story is both fascinating and chilling.

Similarly, I spent some time looking into military executions. Some of those shot had committed crimes, but some who were found guilty of cowardice or desertion were almost certainly suffering from what we now call PTSD. In one case, the soldier, a young man of nineteen, had only been absent for a few hours. He claimed to be suffering from confusion, but he had donned civilian clothes. He was executed, and the whereabouts of his body are unknown. In his hometown, his name has never been added to the war memorial. In another case, the young man was only sixteen years old when he lied about his age to enlist. Later, having seen many of his fellows killed, he left his post to comfort a friend. When he was executed, he was just seventeen; still too young to be a member of his regiment.

It took the British Government ninety years to issue a group pardon to all those who were executed in World War One; a war that was also called The Great War for Civilzation.

On that sombre note, I'll sign off. Thanks again for joining me on this journey. I hope I'll have the pleasure of your company again very soon.

All the best,
Michael Campling
Devon, 2019

Want more like this? Please consider leaving a review.

Reviews are a great way of encouraging authors to write more in a series or a genre, so if you'd like more books like this, your review will support the development of new books. Even a short review will help. Thank you.

While You're Here

Find Out About The Awkward Squad – The Home of Picky Readers:

All members get a free mystery book plus a starter collection at:

mikeycampling.com/freebooks

THE KENNING FAMILY HISTORY

Timothy Kenning marries Hester Williams 1899

Cyril born 1899

Gordon born 1900

Timothy dies in 1905

Cyril awarded the Croix de Guerre 1918

Cyril dies 1919

Gordon marries Diana Muir 1923

Gerald born 1925

Gerald Marries Helen Barker 1947

David is born 1948

David marries Julia Normanby 1968

Martin is born 1969

Deborah born 1970

Gordon dies 1972

Diana dies 1983

Gerald and Helen die 2005

In 2019:

David Kenning is 71

Martin Kenning is 50

Deborah Kenning is 49

ACKNOWLEDGEMENTS

"We will remember them" quote from *For the Fallen* (Robert Laurence Binyon)

"We are returning by the road we came" quote from *To My Brother* (Siegfried Sassoon) Sassoon, Siegfried. The Old Huntsman and Other Poems. New York: E. P. Dutton & Company, 1918; Bartleby.com, 1999. www.bartleby.com/135/.

Special thanks to my excellent beta readers:

Philip

Ilse

Sue

Julie

Saundra

Netty.

ALSO BY MICHAEL CAMPLING

See them all at:

michaelcampling.com

The Devonshire Mysteries

A Study in Stone

Valley of Lies

Mystery at the Hall

Murder Between the Tides (Summer 2020)

ABOUT THE AUTHOR

Michael (Mikey to friends) is a full-time writer living and working on the edge of Dartmoor in Devon. He writes stories with characters you can believe in, and plots you can sink your teeth into. His style is vivid but never flowery; every word packs a punch. His stories are complex, thought-provoking, atmospheric, and grounded in real life.

Michael's work spans several genres and you can explore the full range via his website: michaelcampling.com. Alternatively, you can start reading his work for free with a complimentary mystery book plus a starter library which you'll receive when you join Michael's readers' group, which is called The Awkward Squad. You'll discover free books and stories, plus a newsletter that's actually worth reading. Learn more and start reading today via Mikey's blog at:

mikeycampling.com/freebooks

COPYRIGHT

© 2019 Michael Campling All rights reserved.

No portion of this book may be reproduced in any form without permission from the copyright holder, except as permitted by copyright law.

This is a work of fiction. Names, characters, places, and incidents either are the products of the author's imagination or are used fictitiously. Any resemblance to actual persons, living or dead, businesses, companies, events, or locales is entirely coincidental.

Made in the USA
Coppell, TX
03 September 2020

35868309R00073